WHISPERINGS

WORDSMITHS TULLAMORE

ISBN: 978-1-911131-59-5

This book was published in cooperation with
Choice Publishing, Drogheda, Co. Louth,
Republic of Ireland.
www.choicepublishing.ie

Book Cover Photography by kind permission
of Paul Moore Photography, Tullamore
and Group Photograph by kind permission
of Mary L Dunne.

ABOUT WORDSMITHS

Wordsmiths Tullamore Creative Writers' Group was established in 2017. The group has enjoyed sustained and on-going interest.

Wordsmiths are a voluntary group with a diverse mix of members who meet weekly in Tullamore Library.

- Encouraging one another to write regularly and submit our work for consideration by the group.
- Endeavouring to give positive feedback so that the work can be strengthened and improved.
- Organising events to promote the advancement of our area through literature.
- A token membership subscription of 8 euro per calendar month is payable to cover admin and competition fees; travel to Literary Festivals and Writing Retreats.

AUTHORS

PHILOMENA NEWTON

Biography

Born in Tullamore, County Offaly, a child of the 60s. Former member of Writing Heads and now proud member of Tullamore Wordsmiths. I have been writing poetry for many years and have found it to be a wonderful uplifting way to pass the time. I have a keen interest in all things mystic and love to explore the cosmic map of the soul. I love the complex symbolism in dreams, the inherent mystery in the Tarot and the delightful gifts the universe bestows when we take the time to connect. I love to walk, long walks and commune with ethereal beings. I read extensively. Patrick Kavanagh and Yeats would be my favourite poets. I love all poetry as it is a chance to express oneself in a way that would otherwise seem frivolous. Tullamore Wordsmiths has opened a new world for me.

A circle of pure gold. Healing through sharing soul space, for where we meet, an aesthetic light mending our brokenness and celebrating our uniqueness, a place where miracles happen.

LEAVING

My cases are packed

I am ready to go

The taxi is waiting

I’ve left you a note.

Saying goodbye

For my last time

This house is yours love

The ticket is mine.

Philomena Newton

WHAT I DIDN'T TELL YOU THEN

What I didn't tell you then

As I lived in your abundant womb

I knew a little boy was what you wanted

And he would be coming soon.

What I didn't tell you then

I cannot tell you now

Lost you completely

By the age of ten

You had other fields to plough.

It was a long road

I weep for what might have been

You were too remote

We had a separate dream.

Schooldays full of noise and stuff

Where I was reminded daily

For God I was not enough.

When it came to Communion time

I ate the flattened tasteless bread

the old Priest drank the wine.

Asking questions the teacher could not answer

On reflection was not wise of me

Separating the dance from the dancer

In a spiral dance I tried to free.

I didn't tell you then

I could see the signs were there

I could see the light around you

One you couldn't share.

Boarding School without chat or fuss

You decided was the best for me

The first time I heard my Daddy curse

Imbued with a sadness I could plainly see.

Convent years fell away quick and soon,

Old Sr. Catherine caught me hosting a séance

In the old McAuley room

Somehow caused quite a stir

Asked to explain.

"Sure Sister that's where the Spirits are"

She shouted loud at me

With words of contempt and distain

I wondered why she didn't believe

There is a Spirit in every holy name.

What I didn't tell you then,

What I wanted you to see

I had found a door deep within

I wanted to share with you the key.

You brought me over to the local Jesuits

Grey Old men dressed in chalky black

Where I had to explain

What I was doing

with my treasured Tarot pack.

You didn't like my writing

And the emotions it expressed

You kept on fighting

Until I gave it up

Perhaps it was for the best.

In' 79 you ordered me to see the Pope

I knew then our time had passed

The Stage hanged themselves with Judas rope

The scene was changing fast.

What I didn't tell you then

As you passed into the spirit world

Its too late to tell you now

A great shift has occurred.

Philomena Newton

THE ABC OF LIFE

A is for the alchemy, the power deep within my soul

B is or the breadth in man, bird, tree and stone

C is for the Christ in every man crucified

D is for the old Deities within that can never be denied

E is for the Energy that fuels every atom still

F is for the Fear that tries to break the human will

G is or the Golden Gate, the Solar Plexus divine

H is for the Harp, the music that marks the end of time

I is for the Imagination the gift Adam got with apple seed

J is for the Joy the Imagination experiences from smoking weed.

K is for Karma the stuff that is not supposed to happen

L is for Love, just LOVE the goalpost at the end of every lesson

M is for the Magic the intellect disregards

N is for Nirvana, the feeling the death of intellect rewards

O is for Occult the science that digs deep within for Truth

P is for the Passion it takes to eat forbidden fruit

Q is for Quabbla illuminating the esoteric in sacred scripture

R is for Reincarnation the never ending life imbued in nature

S is for Séance and the joy we get in chasing spirits

T is for Tarot illuminating sacred mysteries beyond our limits

U is for the Umbilical chakra from where the departing soul may escape

V is for Venus the planet upon which the emotion of love may rotate

W is for Wisdom the price for which we pay is youth

X is for the things we kiss away in search of a deeper truth

Y is for the Yin and Yang the basis for all order in this Universe of ours

Z is for Zodiac, the heavenly divisions of earthly hours.

Philomena Newton

Chimney Memories

The passage way for sulphured souls

A reminder that when it comes to belief

We are all alone.

Contaminating the clean air

Reducing humans to palliative care.

The spiral of midnight blue in morning light

Confirming we have made it through the night.

I have heard the Tree Spirits burn

Into the ashes to be returned………….

I remember the Ash spitting out in anger

the old Oak heating our home in weeping slumber,

from the dried Elm recall the sounds

Moans and groans from ancient burial grounds.

And as the turf and ash spluttered in the grate

Old Gods coming to terms with their evolving state.

Our chimney facilitating all of this

Scenting the air the wind has kissed.

Philomena Newton

Golden Moments

Access to

Quantum lighted paths

To unscheduled

Beginnings.

Golden moments

Suffocating time

Tender bitterness

Birthing rhyme

Breathing the fragrance

Of loneliness

Into the scarce days of my now.

Golden moments

Feverishly dancing the spiral dance

Casting momentous doubt.

While I gaze

At the sun,

At the moon,

At the stars

Steering the Plough

While all around me wonder

To what subterranean waters

Has she escaped to this time?

I recall

Golden moments

The great orchestra of emotions fuse

With the rich tapestry of soul

Making me different

Rendering me blind.

Philomena Newton

LET'S THINK ABOUT IT

Let's think about it
Said Adam to Eve
Apples are good for you
Angels are deceived.

Let's think about it
Man of dust and Earth
There is no doubt about it
Woman of Rib superior worth.

Let's think about it
We have the run of the garden
Woman let's think about it
Eating divine apples no pardon.

Let's think about it
I am so utterly bored
I want to believe it
But I am not so sure.

Let's think about it
Said the old serpent with charm
Angels have doubts about it
Sure a wee bite can do no harm.

Let's think about it
Fruit is good, pleasing to the eyes
Eternity, Lets think about it
Far too much Paradise?

Let's think about it
They only had one little bite
While a man on his death bed
May be forgiven
For sinning all his life.

Philomena Newton

THE VISITORS

My first attempt to write a one-act play.

Setting the Scene

A country village in rural Ireland in 1985. Bridget Daly a woman in her late 30s of Bohemian appearance answers her doorbell. On opening the door she mutters "Jesus Christ."

Long-haired stranger standing at the door smiles gently.

Stranger: "Ei that's me."

In a trance she surprises herself by letting the stranger into her dishevelled home.

Bridget: "Whoooo did you say you are? You look kinda strange, then everything does around here looks like (shaking her head) couldn't be just couldn't be (shaky laugh). I must be going mad. Whoo....who.... are you again?"

Stranger: "Jesus is my name. I am a little bit lost today. I was making my way to another galaxy and now I find myself here."

Bridget: Wiping her eyes staring "Who the hell are you, me hearing is a little mad today? I thought you said Jesus."

Stranger: Yes! Yes! You! You recognised me on opening your door.

Bridget: "Jesus Christ!"

Stranger: "That is right."

Bridget: *[muttering]* "I am awake. I am not going mad. God what did I drink last night?"

Stranger: "Two bottles wine, three Vodkas and two pints of cider?"

Bridget: [*reddening]* "That was not a bloodee question"

Stranger: "Oh! I am sorry."

Bridget: "Let me get this straight. You knock on my door. I let you in and you tell me you are Jesus Christ and I am supposed to believe you."

Stranger: "Yes, that's right. Why do you find it so hard to believe me? After all you did recognise me when you opened the door."

Bridget: *[muttering to herself again.]* "This is not happening. This is just a dream [*pinching herself].* I am going to wake up any minute."

Stranger: "I am who I say I am. I have just lost my way."

Bridget: "Lost your way. I thought you were supposed to be The Way. Oh! I really am losing it now. Next thing you will be telling me is that you are coming with good news."

Stranger: "No, I come hungry and I am in need of something to eat, please."

Bridget: *[staring at the man indignantly]* "Something to eat. Something to eat, did you say? Do you see Mary and Martha's Diner written over my feckin' door? Oh! Me head. I am never drinking again, Jesus Christ. Best mind trip I had since that ecstasy pill back in the 80s.

Nah! This is definitely not real. I am asleep. I am going to wake up with one hell of a hangover. Yeah! Its lucid dreaming. I think that's what they call it, or is it lucid dreaming? Some fun so. Really Jesus Christ!"

__Stranger:__ "Yes, Bridget."

__Bridget:__ "O.K! O.K! O.K! I have had enough of this. Prove it."

__Stranger:__ "What?"

__Bridget:__ "I said prove it."

Bridget fills two glasses of water, places them on the table in front of her visitor and says "A merlot and a Chardonnay, please. Let's clear up this lost God business before I lose my mind. Before I lose my already lost mind."

The Stranger places his hands over the glasses; one turns plum red while the other slightly changes.

__Bridget:__ "My God!"

Bridget tastes the liquids, makes a sour face and spits it all out.

__Bridget:__ "That tastes bloodee awful man."

__Stranger:__ "Well the recipe is over 2000 years old."

__Bridget:__ "What did I smoke last night?"

__Stranger:__ "Absolutely nothing my dear."

Bridget: "That was not a bloodee..........oh never mind" I am going to wake up. This is just a dream. I am going to wake up."

Stranger: "Any chance of something to eat. Proving who I am has left me very hungry and tired."

Bridget: "Could fry you a rasher if you like."

Stranger: "Anything else in the house?"

Bridget: "A tin of sardines."

Stranger: "With some bread, a little wine, and perhaps a little cheese what will be fine."

Bridget: "Oh me poor, poor head, never drinking again, oh how I am losing me already lost mind...."

There is a strange kinda knocking at the door..........both listen, Bridget now quite with it, Jesus looking like he knows who it is.

Bridget: "Is someone at the door or is it my mind coming home? Oh my head!.I will never drink again."

Stranger: "There is someone at the door my dear. You have visitors."

The doorbell rings again and a startled Bridget once again answers her door.

Bridget: "Mother! Mother! What the.......what the hell are you doing here?"

Mother: "I have come over to give Jesus a hand."

Bridget: "Christ not you Ma, this is not real. This is not happening, I am not going too mad, and I am going to find my lost mind! I am! Mother you are supposed to be...to be.....well, supposed to be somewhere else?"

Mother makes for the door Bridget jumps out in front of her.

Bridget: "Mother, where do you think you are going?"

Mother: "Just running across the road to chat with Aggie Sullivan."

Bridget: "Oh no you don't! Oh no you don't! Well you can't! Ah ma! For Christ's sake ma! The last time she saw you was fifteen years ago, at your wake."

Philomena Newton

Monologue after Act one

Not quite myself today

It is the drink you see

Or perhaps that Ecstasy pill

I took way back in 1983.

A fella who says he is Jesus

And my long deceased Mother sits

As though it was a normal evening

O my head sure hurts a bit.

Well you did see

He turned water into wine

All the things I couldn't see.

Perhaps he really does heal the blind.

"What am I going to do with the pair of them?

Where can I put them, put them down?

Spare crosses and spare coffins.

Don't come easy in this old forgotton town."

Tell me Jesus why you made it so complicated

Could you have not left us in Eden Wild?

My head and liver too deflated

Feeling like a long lost forgotten child."

"As Columbo might say,

Just one more question,"

"Jesus if you killed your Father

Who would man the gates"?

"I am in the father

And the father is in me

Or so the Good book states."

"Tell me what heaven is like

Will I like it over there"?

"Child, Heaven is ... Heaven is a light

In every person everywhere".

"And why so many laws to keep?"

"Child I only asked for one

Love one another,

And do not create cause for weep

And so your job is done."

"Oh my aching head

I am talking to a ghost

Funny thing about it

He makes more sense than most

Just one more question,

As Columbo would say,

"Was your Mother really a virgin when you were born?

Can you tell me if it is true?"

"Oh Child you have a lot to learn"

Its only faith that dyes the Virgin mantle blue."

"Jesus did she really ascend body and soul into the Clouds"?

"No she didn't child

She is buried in Holy ground."

"And as for the Philosopher's Stone

Well it does not exist at all

Remember child you are never alone

Meditate and you will know it all."

"Do you entertain bad thoughts?"

Said the man from Galilee

"Ha! Ha! Ha! He! No my dear man

Those bad thoughts spend hours entertaining me."

"Thoughts my child are a form of energy

Directing them gets things done

Every vibration has a synergy

Resonating within every holy one.

Just one more question

One before the Good Book bled?

"Do spirits have DNA?

Spirits and DNA...

Not until man can raise the dead.

"Tell me something else man if you have the nerve

Why do women have to cover their head

In order for you to serve?"

And just for the record I would like to point out to you

You have a gypsy's head of hair

and a gypsy's aura about you too."

Oh! I hate it when you smile that smile

Like you understand it all

Oh I need vodka,

And a glass of wine or two,

I need to make a call.

"Hate to bring it up again

But were Mary and Joseph actually man and wife?

"Oh Child my child

Lets not begin again

Yes I have brothers and sisters and a very happy life."

"Ok ok ok so we do our best what then"?

"As brothers and sisters in this universe

We are all each other's next of kin"

"You left us with more questions than answers

Though I know you did your best

And dem Apostles of yours wrote far

Far too many letters

As the good book did attest

They wrote in riddles about a yonder Kingdom

Sure 'tis no wonder no one wrote back to them."

"The answer child is love, unconditional love

The only thing one cannot deface.

And what about all the rules?

"O h child my child there is only one

In living a life of Grace"

Love every man as a brother

Separation is not the norm.

Nor are we born to feed the worm"

"Now Jesus man I have done me homework too

I know there are angels above us

All assigned to you

And when it comes to humans we are number ten

We live we die and do it all again."

"Oh child my child you take it all so to heart

I am in you

You are in me

Heaven is your just reward.

"Its love in every soul that seeks expression

And another thing you might find rather odd

No need for mortal man to hear your confession.

You can talk direct to God."

Fat chance of that

Of anyone hearing my -

My - my confession

"Every heart knows when it fails,

Every heart knows when love is clear

There is no punishment and no gales

No reason to live in earthly fear."

If love breaks your laws

Then your laws are wrong

Take time to pause

There are no laws to make you strong

Earthly law is about control

Eevery nation has had its Toll"

"In wounds that live on through the years

Wounds that will only be healed by Seers

Who can see behind the veil

That there is in fact no God for sale

And its all just a Spin

I am at the centre of the heart that you are living in

They burned your Witches and your Wise

For that the God within me can only apologise

For I have known their bitter fruits

And you in latter times have got acquainted with their rotten roots

Which will be snagged away in wanton cries

For soon, very soon there will be another Paradise!"

Jeseesus..........................."

Philomena Newton

Acknowledgments

This has been such a magnificent journey it is hard to know where to start when acknowledging people who made this happen. Thank you to all my friends in Wordsmiths who share, heal and care for each other so very much. In particular I would like to thank Lorraine Dormer, the gentle genius behind us all encouraging us when we were tired, looking after us and keeping us on the right track throughout this Project. Thank you to my friends Mary Gallagher and Marian Flynn for reading my work and approving it for me. I acknowledge all who have crossed my path and inspired me to write.

....

GERALDINE O'TOOLE

Biography

GERALDINE O TOOLE

A former student of Scoil Mhuire and Tullamore College, Geraldine has been writing poetry since she was a teenager. She later studied English Literature and Philosophy in St. Patrick's University, Maynooth and furthered her studies at All Hallows College, Dublin and St. Patrick's College Carlow, nourishing her interest in Spirituality and Psychology.

Among her achievements Geraldine's work was acknowledged by the Shinrone Poetry Group Competition as highly recommended. She was awarded a writer's residency from Offaly County Council for Tyrone Guthrie Artist Centre, was a contributor to the book 'Spoken Word Writing to be Heard' in 2015 supported by Arden View Resource Centre, Tullamore and as a local poet was asked to and participated in the 'Sharing Stories from Offaly' DVD which was produced in the summer of 2018.

Geraldine writes poetry, prayerful reflections and short stories and her work as a poet and writer continues to flourish under the mentorship of Tullamore Wordsmiths Writers' Group.

Children's Alphabet Poem

Anastasia

Bought

Cian's

Dog

Extra

Food

Good

Houndog

Immediately

Jealous

Kenneth

Left

Moping

Noticing

Over

Peter's

Quilt

Round

Shiny

Tiny

Ultra

Violet

Waggonwheels

X-rated

Zombies

Dedicated to Johnny and Adam Leavy.

Geraldine O'Toole

LIVING

When the physical body becomes steadily and slowly disabled by normal ageing a freedom is unleashed.

Soul has a layer less to wear.

When the adult brain becomes more unreliable and loyally fumbled by natural tiring an innocence is reborn.

Soul has a layer less to bare.

When the human heart becomes scourged and dissected deliberately by jab after jab a joyful threshold is attained.

Soul has a layer less to tear.

Geraldine O'Toole

THE BAD THING

Child: Do you have a cave?

I do.

Child: Why?

It's necessary.

Child: What's inside?

Many shades of colours

Many textures of earth.

Child: Oh....is it big?

It's vast and claustrophobically minute.

It's a changeable cave. Is mine.

Child: Who else knows?

One or two.

Child: Where is it?

In my heart.

Child: In my heart.

Child: Cave in your heart?

Tell me about it.

A bad thing happened a long time ago. I was very scared.

Life grew grey quickly.

I slept a lot then.

I spoke very little.

I caved in.

The pieces of me were many.

The bad thing caused me to shatter.

I fell apart....into a damp emotionless cave.

I knew nothing for sure

The guaranteedness of living shifted beneath my feet

I fell endlessly down between many worlds

Cave time stole me from myself

I evolved backwards into a Neolithic warrior.......A Gerosaurus of sorts.

My animal instincts drew me to hibernate in cave

With supplies of pills, sugary stuff, music and the melancholic dark

I kind of died.

Diagnoses draped itself around me

Evil laughter rocked my refuge

Engulfed in a deluge of tears

I hated cave-time.

I hated a lot then.

Hate sucked deliciously life's essence from me.

Long. Long......

After all of this

Cave brightened

I was surprised

In disbelief, suspicious

Seeds of joy, small, yet ever present took to cave's damp soil and yielded a decent crop

Cave improved.

I learned it is o.k. to be in darkness.

I learned it is o.k. to be in brightness.

Cave time teaches.

Cave time stretched me.

In retrospect cave time me.

This poem I dedicate in gratitude to AWARE Support Group in Tullamore.

AWARE for people living with the challenges of mental health.

Geraldine O'Toole

LADY McDERMOTT FROM DURROW

It is seemingly so simple to look upon you and dream immediate thoughts of inner beauty.

You inflame cherished desires within the depths of my most obscure and undeserving heart.

I am wishing to describe to my unconscious state of mind felicitous verbs in order to paint a permanent picture of your countenance there.

Alas! My attempts at seeking out perfect syllables have been numbed.

I am in relaxed awe of your pure and archetypal beauty.

My abilities to express any appreciation of such a divinely treasure as you, madam are left totally inchoate and in my naivety I feel worthless in front of you.

I cherish every graceful and innocent movement.

I long to embrace you and slowly unfurl the abundant falling tresses of your tender curling hair.

The mischievous spray of freckles on your peachey complexion.

The trail of almost transparent dust particles as you thrust by in a gay attempt to avoid any mortal conversation with me, me – the one who loves you so dearly and sincerely from an imprisoned distance

Childishly smiling and peacefully playing with the ardent affections of my heart;

My poor and tiring heart.

Madam, you are the ailment of no cure.

Nightly you I lure with untold weight in my nocturnal fantasies.

You are the constant content of my dreams under the emptiness of my quilt I should prefer one silent kiss, one silent kiss.

Than the recurring cold of a thousand sleepless nights.

Dedicated to my Grandmother, Mary McDermott.

Geraldine O'Toole

WHO AM I?

I am she of Celtic descent.

I am ark and I am covenant.

I am nature spirit soul and being.

I am hearing sensing loving feeling.

I am lined with waking womb.

I am Mother and child entombed.

I am slave and master freed.

I am forest I am seed.

I am breathing...

I am giving.

I am female happy in this knowing.

I am thief and I am giver.

I am warm and I am shiver.

I am night and I am day.

I am autumn.

I am May.

I am blossom.

I am petal

I am soil and I am nettle.

I am colours of the rainbow.

I am days when I don't know.

I am Penelope I have waited.

I am Ophelia I have been fated.

I am Venus.

I am love.

I am woman.

And I am dove.

Geraldine O'Toole

TOWARDS A PLACE OF STRENGTH

Da, on the bog working at the turf.

Why did Mammy love you so?

How come you happened to be so lovely?

It makes missing you so painful.

Memory brought you back to me and;

I saw you with your blue shirt rolled up and your sun tanned arms moved and stretched as you turned the sods

Your hard hand resting on the turf tools, slapped upright

In the wettin' sogginess of the bog's bank as your other hand held your fag, and you'd make that quare crooked face

As you dragged the life out of the 'fag'.

Sweat beads gathered under your nostrils

And were wiped away in ferociousness,

As you'd spit out the phlegm coughing juices of tar

From all the hard work, bog dust

And the previous million and one fags you'd have over the years.

As I aged twelve with plaited neatly divided hair

Looked on in my innocence.

I worked with you on the bog

On those Saturday afternoons.

I knew in my own unknown knowledge

How much in love with the bog you were even then.

The spirit of the bog still touches me too.

I'm glad it does.

Her gentle presence;

She just is.

She gets cut and sliced up and sold

And so do people.

The sweet sound of summer sun

And the moist scent of warm wind is musical to me

What a freshness there is on our bog

Ballard Bog, thrown out upon the lands between Tullamore Town and Killurin countryside.

Its Irish, it's pure

It reminds me of you.

You were my image of God.

You were my strength

My backbone

At times I use 'stubbornness'

That trait so synonymous with the 'O'Tooles'

That trait you had yourself, and were known for it.

Thank God.

Oh my heart leaps with pride for my name and yours

And we are connected with a spirit of similarity

And mutual love for places of quiet and peace

The bog was your Cathedral

That was where you prayed in honest earnestness

The church of the poor. I understand that now

The banks from which we cut was the altar

And our Eucharist was the few loaves of O'Shea's bread

Mammy packed in the rush on Saturday mornings

We celebrated our work, the good weather, the progress made

Before the rains fell and the friendships we shared by being family.

Dedicated to Ma & Da, Denis, Joan, John and Libby

Geraldine O'Toole

THE LONGEST DAY 21st June 2018

Seven-thirty a.m. waken up, sunny and windy, a bright combination. My son ready for surgery, hoping to breathe with more success and less pain. Trusting this day, that has been long anticipated. Hospital checking in, answering questions, the banter with nursing staff, Kevin hungry and happy. We are invited to take a seat in the waiting area, a kitchenette filling up with fasting children and coffee sipping parents.

We sit apart. I choose a stool. He the sole armchair. The phone comes out. Scrunched up the intense interaction commences. Teenager and his world.

A girl aged eight or nine seated beside her Dad catches my attention. Soft ballet shoes, long flowing skirt, loose pink top, in a world of her own. On the table in front of her, is laid a white napkin, upon which are neatly made figures from plasticine. Green, lilac, white, red and brown. Her bag full and noisy with the wrappings of other colours. She works with her fingers; a rose mounted on purple background, tiny green leaves at its centre. She coughs, suggesting bronchial issues. Her tall Dad, focused on her creation leans towards her looking supportively. Taking her work closer up towards her eyes she looks intent for a few silent serious moments, then begins the rework. She smooths out, re-engraves, and curls skinny legs under her. A comfort and immersion evolve she is in her work at one with it.

Her tools are a pen, and a broken plastic tea spoon, sharp edge defining the faces on her work. Exacting expressions and intricate details.

Quietness abruptly pierced by a loud nurse questioning *"Ella?"*. Dad relieved, lifts up Ella's bag and prepares to pack up her creations. In an attempt to make eye contact I break the waiting silence and tell her "Your work is beautiful." She looks at me, smiles and says faintly "Thank you." We saw one another.

I welcomed a nod from her father. Ella is encouraged towards a weighing scales. Directions from the nurse are precise. "Stand tall now Ella and don't move." They collect their things hurriedly. Some of Ella's pieces fall from her gathered napkin. I hear a shocked sigh. "Oh no!", and a wheeze leaves her chest as she bends to the floor instantly. "It's o.k." the nurse retorts Ella, "you can pick those up afterwards, I just need to weigh you now."

Ignoring the nurse, Ella continues to pick up her treasured pieces of work as, indeed, would anyone. And the notion strikes loudly in my heart....

Who wouldn't stoop to rescue the thing they love?

On the floor Ella's legs are lost beneath her bellowing skirt. Dainty fingers pick and place her work into the napkin on her lap. They are safe now. Ella has a few uneasy breaths. She remains until composed enough to take her stand. Dad keenly looks at Ella, he waits, she passes all her work up into his large hands, and he receives them carefully, respectfully. Ready, she steps on the scales. Figures noted by the impatient nurse. They disappear down the corridor towards theatre.

Kevin is next to be called. Turning the phone off we follow the nurse. The waiting area was inspirational. Later we watched plasticine modelling tutorials on his phone. But I had earlier met the best.

Geraldine O'Toole

MARTHA McMAHON

My Father Was a Big Man

Emergence

ABC List of Poets Worth a Look [Up]

Storm Cloud

Waste Was A Word Unheard of Yet

Savannah

My First Day at School

Christmas 1977

Biography

A member of Wordsmiths Tullamore and from Kilbeggan, Co. Westmeath, where she lives with her husband and four children. Martha McMahon is a writer and poet with a gentle narrative.

My Father Was a Big Man

My Father was a big man,
although at five-foot three
those who knew him might disagree.

He had broad shoulders,
the perfect seat for me,
to sit while he drank his tea.

He'd drive home from work,
in a blue car, wearing blue overalls
that smelt of oil.

He'd eat his dinner
and let me eat from his plate,
new potatoes with butter, tasted great,
at six I could eat six,
at seven he was in heaven,
so my Father remained a big man.

My Father had big hands,
My Mother said he hadn't hands to hammer a nail,

but my Father's hands could hold a microphone,
get a tune from a fiddle,
play the drums or the accordion,
they could dig in the garden,
and accept a bottle of diluted orange,
they could drive us to the lake,
they could join in prayer,
they could salute and wave to everyone he knew,
they could lift me up.
My Father's big hands could hold mine.

Martha McMahon

Emergence

Taking to the stage,
Reading her part,
Engaging with the audience,
Accepting the applause,
So it is, she is reborn.

A kind of exuberance now,
No return,
Incarnation of new self,
Creative insight awakened.

Honing her craft,
Orator with confidence,
Raconteur with ease,
Master of disguise,
Acclaimed artiste.

Introspection recalls...
Came from nothing.

Martha McMahon

ABC List of Poets Worth a Look

*"**A**dversity is the first path to truth"* said

Byron famous British poet apparently the romantic sort

*"**C**ould I but ride indefinite, as doth the meadow-bee, and visit only where I*

liked and no man visit me" wished.

Dickenson, so many, so sad, so morbid, but must be perused.

Emily Bronte, another Emily, wistful words that beg to be heard such as:

***F**aith and Despondency "The winter wind is loud and wild, Come close to me, my darling child;"*

Goldsmith, famous for his deserted village, yet I found out there's more to him than that

Heaney of course, were it not alphabetical would be top of my list

"on winter evenings.
With pails and barrows
those mound-dwellers
go waist-deep in mist"

*"**I** hear an army charging upon the land"*, who knew?

James Joyce famous for Ulysses was indeed, a poet too.

Kavanagh now there's a poet I had actually read

"**L**ines Written on a Seat on the Grand Canal Dublin" is just one, but my advice is don't leave out one, least you miss a line like this ....for me equalled by none

"The light between the ricks of hay and straw Was a hole in Heaven's gable"

Mansfield Katherine, to give this fine lady a mention, her poem "A Fine Day" worthy of contention

Native Irish speakers will enjoy the works of

"**O**' Riardain Sean, when he writes about the "Local Happenings"

Percy Shelly, to study his, would take one to a higher plane, when he wrote about

Quite, in "The Spirit of Solitude" I felt privileged to have read it, so read it again.
Rumi, not perhaps as well known – A Persian Sunni Muslim Poet – I have a beautiful grandniece named after him – his words are sublime- a noble way to start your day such as
"**S**top acting so small, you are the universe in ecstatic motion"
Tennyson another Lord I have chosen for you, can't truly call yourself a wordsmith till you have read a few,..........like
Ulysses a poem penned by he in 1833 long before Joyce's work in 1918 came into being.
Venus described as *"an evening star"* has made the list ....from
William Wordsworth, it would be a travesty if any of his were missed
Xanadu near Kubla Khan another one I have
Yet to read, is in there, ...by Samuel Taylor Coleridge, when I am more intellectually aware,
Zealot, I, long to devour these wordy tomes, upon the banquet table, couplets sonnets verses and poems, feasting *ad infinitum* as long as I am able

Martha McMahon

Storm Cloud

Sun slowly sinking into the waters of Lough Rí, setting in a perfect arc,

the sky darkens and the waves take on the appearance of oil,

on looking skyward, towards the clouds, the lord's face has made a cameo,

reminding me, that he was there, long before, our Celtic *Brian Boru.*

many storms come in life to test, feeling lost at times, but never abandoned.

Martha McMahon

Waste Was a Word Unheard of Yet

The countryside is full of wood pigeon's; you don't have to look for them, they are not inclined to hide. Although breeding all year round, August, it seems, is the preferred month for the baby chicks to hatch, more born in this month than any other. This morning I awaken to a husky Whoo! Hoo! Hoo! the call of the wood pigeon. This call is loud enough to encroach upon my dreams and waken me from slumber. Slowly my ear tunes in to the delicate cacophony of the other birds' subtle morning recital. They are surely getting tired now, from all that chirping, as its long past dawn by the time I am awake. I only have to move my head and look out of my window to study nature's little alarm clock that has me so wide awake and ready to face the day ahead.

The proud and cocky wood pigeon, so self-assured, he attempts to impress his lady friend who thus far hasn't seemed all that interested in his intricate flying routine and loud flapping of wings. It's early still and I have time to really study him. What an elaborate suit of clothes he wears today to go about his work. He looks for all in the world as if he is wearing an old suit of clothing, a grey top coat over a dusky pink jumper with a white collared shirt peeping out, and suddenly my mind drifts back to my grandfather who would have certainly donned similar attire to work in the fields. His old working clothes consisted of his once good suit, which having served him well for many years would not be considered good enough to be called Sunday best, so would now take on a secondary role and be worn as a type of uniform to go about his daily chores, even in the Summer the day would begin with the top coat on and this would be removed later when both he and the day warmed up. There would be the odd day in the summer when making cocks of hay with a pitch fork that the jumper would be removed the sleeves of the white shirt rolled up and if it was particularly sunny a knotted handkerchief would take the place of the woollen peaky cap

My grandfather's shirt would also have had many incarnations, having begun its life, too, as a Sunday best. With stiff starched collar, it would be worn to Mass on Sunday, carefully removed after Mass as all good clothes were and returned to the wardrobe for another week. However, even with all this minding, the collar would eventually become frayed and then my grandmother would carefully remove it and expertly re-sew it turning the collar to consign the frayed piece underneath, never to see the light of day and let my grandfather down at Mass. Nobody would know that this was not a shirt worthy of the occasion. This collar too would eventually fray and this time my grandmother would remove the collar altogether and this shirt would take its place among the ranks of the working shirt. Good quality cotton, it would soften from all the washing and wearing undoubtedly lose its pockets and eventually qualify as a suitable candidate as a night shirt. Finally having served my grandfather well it would be time to harvest the buttons which would be placed in the cardboard Dairy Milk box with the faded purple ribbon to wait along with a plethora of mixed buttons for the day to come when they may be of use once more. Any remaining usable cotton would be carefully cut and rolled into bandages or rags for cleaning, waste was a word unheard of yet.

Martha McMahon

Savannah (Cab Sav)

I wish I had told you that it was a fake, a copy, I saw you take up my soft black leather bag and trace the badge with your fingers wistfully. I know you thought it was the real deal, a Mulberry. I'd say you were one of the few people at Fergal's wedding that would have recognised the label. It was convincing, you believed it, so were you, you had us all fooled for a long time. I could have told you, why did I not? Was it my ego? Did I want you to think it was real? Or was I afraid that if I told you, you might pick up that I sensed a vulnerability in you, fragility underneath that facade and that somehow your mask was beginning to slip. In hindsight I think I was complicit, in the dangerous game you were playing with us all, this game that in the end led to your demise.

I often think back to the circumstance that threw us together, three Irish girls as green as grass, studying in Liverpool. Fate put us in the same house, Fergal was advertising for housemates and what he got was a motley crew. Even when we all went our separate ways we were like family, we still managed to keep in touch, this was years before social media or even e-mail. I remember it was you who gave Fergal the nickname Frugal because he was so careful with money and could live so cheaply. Only for him managing things so well I don't think we would have survived at all. Your nickname was 'Cab Sav', a play on your name and your favourite tipple, Cabernet Sauvignon, it was what we would shout at you at the end of the night, if we saw you snogging some guy we knew you wouldn't be seen with in the clear light of day. We would shout 'Cab Sav' and you would come running as if late for your taxi. Do you remember the night you snogged Fergal? It broke his heart when you married Len. I still can't believe he didn't go to your wedding. We all went to his. He was the last of our bunch to get married. You always said it was because he never found anyone rich enough, I always thought he was holding out for you.

It was the best night we had together, Fergal's wedding. Our last but none of us knew it. You looked amazing in that red dress, your flawless makeup your shiny blonde hair, your big blue eyes, your best feature, we danced and laughed a lot, you didn't need a drink to have a good time, you really were the life and soul of the party and everyone had a better time because you were there. Nobody dared speak about where you had been, even to each other. Everyone knew but nobody admitted it. How would things have turned out if every time you met someone that night they said "Savannah you look amazing? You must be so proud of yourself. It takes a very strong person to pull themselves out of the fire. We are proud of you. We love you. Nobody judges you", or ever judged you". Sadly that wasn't your way; our way. It was easier for everyone to go along with the charade, but then, the music stopped.

You were a magnificent painting, a masterpiece to be viewed, admired and appreciated from afar. Up close or under a magnifying glass you didn't make sense. You were the brightly coloured kite of your family flying high for all to see. The only girl, your brothers the little bows that trailed along behind. Had anyone gently pulled on that kite string and drawn you down to earth, they would have seen, that up close the colours were not so strong and vibrant, they would have seen the little holes and the tears and they would know that one strong gust of wind would be all it would take to rip you apart. Your brothers the little bows, made of stronger stuff, still perfectly formed, colours radiant they thrived out of the glare of expectation. Sadly, grounded now, for however long it takes them to have the courage to soar once more, without you out front.

Martha McMahon

Savannah

You had a beautiful name, exotic even.
Living with that name couldn't have been easy,
there would have been a lot of expectation there,
you made it look easy.

A role you were born to play Savannah, destined to it even.
But what was to be your destiny?
You loved drama but your demise was tragic,
although I couldn't imagine you old,
that would never have suited you.

You were glamorous, movie star chic,
you could never grow old gracefully,
your hair would always be blonde.

You could don the coat of mundane and make it look classy,
you were the master of disguise.
You hid your demons well, even you believed it.
You couldn't ask for help,
you were in competition with us all, though we didn't know.

We never would have wanted to play anyway,
we were just trying to get through the same as you.
We loved your beautiful self,
you were irreverent and we forgave you,
you were so funny and we adored you.

You had a kind and generous heart..... a weak one,
it didn't take much.
You didn't believe you could live, I wish you could have.

You gave so much, although you didn't value your contribution.
You thought you were a failure, if your life wasn't perfect.
You beat yourself up in your head, for failing life's tasks.
You combusted before our eyes, a fire we couldn't put out.

There was too much fuel, all we could do was stand and watch.
It was a slow burn, but too out of control to do anything about it.
When the fire died, so did you,
and your beauty was there, pure for all to see,
to remember, to lament, your life spent.

Martha McMahon

My First Day at School

Looking back, I think she did me a disservice when my Mother allowed me to have a nap around noon each day. But with hindsight when I reflect I think perhaps the nap was more for her than for me. I was the youngest of six children born almost twenty years after her first child. We were relatively evenly spaced out with about four years between each of us on average. It must have seemed to my Mother that when she put a child on the school bus for the first time, she would return to the house and there would be a new baby. Not this time though, when my turn came there was an empty house waiting. I wonder did she do a highland fling. or was she a little sad? My money is on the first. I often wistfully looked at the school bus stopping at our front gate to collect my older brother Joe and my sister Josephine, wishing that I too could take that magical journey. The yellow bus was the biggest thing I had ever seen, bigger I am sure than Sonny's lorry, the only other large vehicle to grace our country road on the way to the nearby sandpit.

My day finally did come I boarded the bus with my sister and brother. I showed my bus ticket to the bus driver Frank. I remember feeling it. There was a strange texture to it. It felt as if there were pieces of cotton thread stuck to the outside. I really wanted to pick at the threads, but my sister intervened and removed the ticket to her care and out of my inquisitive fingers. I must have been wearing a dress or skirt as I can remember the cold of the plastic seats on the bus on my skin, even though it was not cold outside being September. I also remember being gently reprimanded by my sister for tasting the silver chrome bar that you were meant to hold onto. I looked around and felt relieved to see that Connie our friend and neighbour was also on the bus.

The bus drove past our gate and headed in a direction to my knowledge I had never been before. The only journeys made by me up to this point, had always required going out the gate and turning right. To Mass on a Sunday morning to visit our Granny, or to the doctor on the back of Mam's bike. The bus took no length to arrive at its destination; I would find out later that being the last people picked up meant that you were the last people to be dropped off. The bus journey home that evening, was literally the longest journey of my short life. My brother now eight years old, was dropped at the boy's school, I would enter my new school by the wrong door and ensure my bearings were completely lost; this was because my sister who was by now in first year in the adjoining secondary school had wanted to show me off to her school friends. I have a vivid memory of running so fast down the long corridor to my new classroom that I was lifted off the floor by Josie and her friend Geraldine as I was unable to keep up. I was late on my very first day.

The door handle of junior infants was large and oval in shape. It was metal, dark brown in colour and cold to the touch, it was also stiff and difficult to open as it was so large for my small hand. The floor was gleaming, shiny wooden floorboards, I would later become adept at cleaning wooden floors during my convent education and learn to love the smell of floor polish, but this would come much later. I would also wear slippers in school as all my school friends did until we were 17 or 18 years old. Being four years of age however and it being your first day at school, were no mitigating factors when it came to being disciplined for being late. I had to share my double seat with a boy.

To this day I can remember the smell that filled my nostrils, a smell so alien to me that first time, but so familiar to me now upon entering any national school classroom since. It was that pungent aroma of crayons mixed with school books and lunches. I took my seat as instructed but immediately had to stand up as it was time for prayers. The seat was raised and we turned around to face a huge framed picture of 'Our Lady'. She was beautiful, dressed in white, with a long blue cloak, standing on the world with little silver stars on it, she had bare feet and worryingly for me she was standing on a number of snakes. She wore a crown made of thorns or flowers those details escape me but the snakes are clear as day. We were saying the Memorare a long complicated prayer for little children, the meaning escaped me for many years, but I grew to love it long after I had learned it by heart.

It was now time to turn around sit back down and look at our teacher. She was a nun, dressed in black complete with veil. She had a nice face and spoke while smiling, even when she said things that weren't nice. I remember thinking she looked young. She called the role in Irish, you got one chance to remember your name, and it was frightening and confusing. The class despite being mixed was quiet and shy. Unruly behaviour would not be tolerated, this was clear. There was the most exciting melee when one child simply did not want to stay at school and made it abundantly clear to Sister by kicking her on the shins. Her Mother left her third child at school, who soon found out that she didn't have a say in the matter, she and I would remain firm friends for decades to come.

I took in my surroundings, there were magnificent horse chestnut trees in the distance, and you could see them out any of the huge windows which were all along one side of the classroom. This view would accompany my education for the next fourteen years. I would spend many hours daydreaming looking at them in the years to come. They always gave comfort to a dreamer like me. The ceilings were high; there was a large blackboard, an abundance of white chalk and a sparse supply of coloured chalk. There was a small hatch in the wall, which had a handle on it. There was one in every classroom. I always wondered what was in there. Eight years later, when I was in sixth class, I got my answer, the new principal opened the hatch in her class room and made a telephone call.

I was delighted to see a black and white teddy on a shelf and a lovely doll with the word babóg written under it in beautiful handwriting. I would later learn the meaning of the word and also that those toys were to be looked at and not played with. Babóg never moved but occasionally teddy was walked by Sister to a tune, tá teddy ag súil, tá teddy ag súil, hey ho mo Daidaí oh, tá teddy ag súil, teddy would sometimes rith (run) or leim (jump) and it was a pretty effective way to learn Irish vocabulary. Although we didn't get to play with babóg and teddy, there were plenty of things to occupy our little hands and minds. There were short wooden rectangular bricks, you could build with them; they tasted sharp not very pleasant and felt a bit sticky, I think I was not the only one tasting them. There were tiny little slates and tiny pieces of chalk, balls of Marla blended to a dull grey colour, I can still recall the smell and taste even though I tasted only once, there were little boxes full of large ice lolly sticks, again for building with and strengthening your hand muscles for writing later on I guess. My favourite thing by far was a huge baby bath full of the softest sand I had ever felt. There were containers to fill and spill and the sand through my fingers felt like soft velvet. It made me want to suck my thumb, later my wet thumb attracted a lot of sand and when I put that back in my mouth I didn't make the same mistake again.

I can vividly remember the smell of my teacher. She smelled different, I only had one reference point my Mam, and Sister didn't smell like Mam. Mam smelled like perfume although it was most likely scented talcum powder and on the few Saturday nights that she and Daddy went out, her face smelled nice and her lipstick smelled nice and her hair smelled nice, Sister smelled different, not bad, just different. I observed her closely and I never once saw her enter or leave the toilet, I never ever saw her eat anything, so I decided there and then that nuns were a different species, in my four-year-old mind, there were men, women and nuns. Around my noon nap time at home I felt sleepy on my first day at school. I began to slide the brass door over and back to hide the inkwell. It must have had a hypnotic affect as I was soon off, pretty soon I felt a bony knuckle and a smiley face telling me I wasn't a baby and to wake up.

Lunch time was spent out in the yard. There was a long bench in the shed and this is where we sat to eat our lunch. I am pretty sure I had cheese sandwiches and cocoa every day, the cocoa tasted good, replenished my soul and reminded me of home. On my first school day however, I hadn't a clue how to open my new flask, thankfully my kind and gentle friend Connie was there to help me. She was three years older than me and four years ahead of me, a seasoned professional when it came to school. She would later become a wonderful national school teacher herself in that very school, and would be my guardian angel there before she departed for secondary and my guardian angel in life later, when she departed again all too soon.

Martha McMahon

Christmas 1977

Christmas wasn't far away we knew, because Santy wrote to us and told us. Not all the kids mind, no, just the kids in Cumminstown. I don't know why that was, it might have been because Eiley Coffey a neighbour living in England knew someone working in the post office in Lapland and passed on the names, we were so lucky. Getting those letters with the purple fancy writing was so exciting. The letter would be brought on the school bus and compared with our neighbour Connie's, yes of course, she got one too.

It would soon be time for Connie's Mother, Nancy, to come over to our house to help Mammy make the cake. All the exotic smells, mixed spice, grated lemon and orange rind, mixed peel Aunty Vera's cookery book, it was easy to find the page, the book almost parted itself on the right page, a page stained from years of use. Almonds soaking in hot water, to be peeled by Joe and the stickiness of the glace cherries which had to be cut in half by me, lining the cake tin, circles and greaseproof paper and brown paper by my sister Josephine and then the smell, oh the smell when it baked in the oven for hours and hours. You had to be very quiet or the cake would sink. A good many days later the Christmas cake would be iced first with almond icing and later with real royal icing which took forever to make, glycerine what a word, it would be decorated with spikes and a fancy cake band, a plastic snowman on top both brought from Dublin by Marian, sometimes I would be allowed put silver balls on top, not too many, stop, it's the cake not the tree.

If Nancy came for Mammy then Connie came for us, me and my brother Joe when it was time to write the letters. That was good because she had the ruler and markers with all the lids on and we would spend a night drawing the best picture we could, of Santy his sack, his sleigh and Rudolph on the outside and on the inside, in our very best handwriting what we wanted for Christmas presents. The letters were duly burned in the fire to arrive down Santy's chimney in the form of coloured smoke. Santy was great though, he never brought us what we asked for, no, and he brought us what we really wanted. I remember the last Christmas in Cumminstown 1977, I got a post office set, Josie played with me, she liked it too I think, I also remember getting a Cinderella jigsaw in a round tin, Daddy borrowed the tin the next day to hunt the wren.

The milkman did his part, oh the excitement when the foil milk bottle tops turned up with holly printed on them for the month of December. The postman had more sweets than ever, presents no doubt from his rounds at Christmas, toffee éclairs; I remember the rich taste of the chocolate and toffee, what a treat. Mammy would finally give in and let Daddy take down the decoration box from the attic. He would put a candle on a saucer to see what he was doing and let me have a peek in the attic, but only if I promised not to stand anywhere but on the joists The box came down and yes Peter the eldest' first baby bottle was still there along with his first tin box of powder. The tinsel for the tree, the foil decorations for putting on the ceiling of the sitting room corner to corner by my sister Una. When the tree went up, it always had coloured lights and my favourite decoration by far was a purple ball which I would spin and watch hypnotised as the lights of the tree twinkled and I smelled the unfamiliar fresh tree in the house. Daddy would bring home an arm full of holly, I can smell that too. I can vaguely remember seeing a turkey hanging upside down on the back of a door.

Christmas eve, Peter who worked on the busses in Dublin, brought home little double decker busses with sweets in them for me and Joe, we were small enough to creep in between the legs of the glass case in the sitting room where they were hidden underneath and eat a few before they were officially given to us. Another candle on a saucer, this time in the window to welcome the baby Jesus. Recalling the night Myranda our dog saved us all, when the candle set the net curtain on fire one Christmas eve long ago, this story told every Christmas eve. Time now for me and Joe to get the biggest school socks we could find belonging to Josie and hang up for Santy. Mammy making stuffing and roast potatoes. Me and Joe leaving a bottle of stout for Santy and water out on the step for Rudolph, looking up at the night sky one last time, it won't be long...

Snow never came on Christmas day but when it did, it was very welcome. Socks on our hands to make snowmen and snowballs, wellies that didn't keep out the cold but were terrific for sliding on the road, staying out too long so you had to put your feet in the oven to warm up. The tingling when they did. Drying off and going over to the neighbours Cloonans, getting into manure bags and sliding down the hill, snow water getting into the bag and soaking you, finally going home, to warm up, feet in the oven again....

Martha McMahon

Acknowledgements

Thank you to the best family in the world, my family:

Born into....
Married into...
Gave life to....

Thank you to my Wordsmiths family it was great fun to as Sue Boland said ***'hold hands and jump'.*** Particular thanks to Lorraine Dormer, without whom there would have been no book.

Thank you to my family at home and my *work* family, who listened to my submissions and helped me to make selections for the book.

Sincere thanks to Tullamore Library for providing such a lovely space which allows 'the magic to happen' week after week.

Finally, a word of thanks to writer Pauline McNamee, the inspiration behind Wordsmiths Tullamore, your encouraging words reverberate soundlessly at every meeting of the wordsmiths

Martha McMahon

VINCENT HUSSEY

Biography

VINCENT HUSSEY

Vincent was born in Bawnboy, Tralee, in 1944.
Married Pauline Duffy from Killimor, Co. Galway in 1969.
They moved to Tullamore in 1974.
They have five grown-up children.
Worked with Offaly Co. Council for 31 years.
Vincent commenced writing in 2012.
Attended Pauline McNamee's creative writing workshop in 2016 in Tullamore library.

Pauline encouraged us to write "badly" but to write.

Joined Wordsmiths Tullamore writing group in 2017. Wordsmiths provides a safe haven and nurtures us all to explore our talents. It is also great fun!

Vincent's writing is based mostly on old family stories, social history and times past.

Detonators

Boy! Was I sorry that I ever said anything about the detonators?

It was during the Easter Holidays, 1952. My next door neighbour and best friend, Liam, was a year and a day older than myself. We were at a loose end so we sauntered down the field to "Gallowsfields." A horrible name!

The origin of the name was a mystery to us. It was a name that conjured up a harrowing past.
It was a town land of 100 acres. The Urban Council bought about sixty of these and promptly changed the name to "St. Brendan's Park."

My cousins Paddy, Sean and Donal lived there in a railway cottage. Donal, Liam and I were in the same class at school. Sean was a year ahead while Paddy was two years further ahead again. It was a great gathering spot for us young ones. Their parents, Peggy and Tom were very tolerant. Tom was great fun. He was a stone mason on the railway. His brother "Dinny" was his "mate". They were my father's first cousins. Their Mother was his aunt. Their father "old Thady" had been the railway yard boss. He was responsible for a large workforce. He got my father a job on the railway. He was also my father's best man when he married my Mother in 1919. My father spent a lot of time, while he was single, in their house and he contributed to the household expenses. When Money, Tom's sister emigrated, my father subbed her fare to New York. As a child I didn't understand any of that but noticed that there was a strong bond between them.

Two railway lines ran out from town by their cottage for about a mile and a half to the "Junction". There they separated. The branch line ran west to a seaport while the other continued northwards.

We had only moved a few months earlier from a railway cottage on the branch line. My family had occupied the railway cottage rent free for twenty eight years. I was only present for the last six of these years. My Mother actually received one pound £1 (one pound) a year for tending the gates on the adjoining level crossing. The cottage had no water supply and was distant from town. My Mother was overweight, suffered from Arthritis and had high blood pressure. The doctor bluntly warned my Mother that the journey to town was too much for her.

"Woman, you should be dead after that journey in your condition" he scolded her. She got such a fright that she lost over a stone in weight. It was clearly time to shorten the journey!

The Urban District Council built a large scheme of three bedroom houses, with hot and cold running water, and indoor bathrooms in Gallowsfields. The County Council, not to be outdone, built another large scheme on the outskirts of town in the Strand Road area. My preference was for the Gallowsfields site because it was in the Rock Street area and beside the railway. There were three senior football teams in the town - the Rock was our area and club loyalties ran deep.

The council renamed the estate "St. Brendan's Park." The scheme proved very costly so rents were very high while the other scheme was much more affordable. My father said that he couldn't afford the rent. Tom, Bill, Chris and Sam were all working and said they would "chip in "to pay the rent. So we moved to the "Park". Because the rents were so high the council opened tenancy to all and sundry. We had an eclectic mix of residents. We had two secondary school teachers, one of whom scared us; four Technical School teachers; one brilliant primary school teacher; at least a dozen Gardai; four detectives; two engineers; the post master; many tradesmen; two shops; several public servants, several self employed people and a few like ourselves who struggled to pay the rent.

My father refused to move. His excuse was that you couldn't have a good fight because the neighbours would hear! He and one of the dogs and the cat remained behind. My Mother went out each day to cook his dinner, light the fire and do other chores. She returned to town at night to cater for the rest of us. After three weeks he relented and joined us.

The move suited me. In the cottage I was isolated. I was the only one from the area who went to school in town. I missed the boys from the country but two of their families also moved but to the other scheme and consequentially to a different school. My new next door neighbour was in the same class in school and we quickly became best friends.

My father still had the key of the cottage which he used as a store. He and his gang ate there whenever they were in the vicinity.

Detonators were the most exciting thing stored there. My companions never heard of detonators. So I explained them to the boys. They were circular in plan shape. Their diameter was about the size of the lid of a one pound jam jar. They were about half an inch in depth; made of metal and filled with an explosive substance probably gun powder. They could be fixed to the rails with a flexible lead strip and when a train went over them they "went off". They were often called "fog signals" because they could be used as a hazard warning in poor visibility during foggy weather. Mostly they were used for celebratory purposes. If the county team won the All Ireland then a series of them would be placed under the train bringing the triumphant team home. The team always travelled by train and they were regularly triumphant. They were also set off if a railwayman (there were very few women working on the railway in those days) got married. The boys decided they wanted to see the detonators.

None of us knew that they were dangerous when they exploded.

I explained to the boys that the cottage had three rooms consisting of a kitchen and two bedrooms. The bedrooms had wooden floors. A number of rats had tunnelled under the house and up through the floor boards in the back bedroom. My father and his gang had set a ring of rat traps around the hole in the floor. Two rats were caught by the haunches at the one time and they attacked each other. My father and the gang found them alive and cruelly killed them.

Back to us; Liam's father was a Carlow man and his Mother was from town, a real "townie". Liam had always lived in town and so was not familiar with rat traps. We found a rusty rat trap one day in the field at the end of the road we lived on. I explained how it worked.

"You set the trap by opening the jaws and then press them in position. Then you place the bait on that tray between the open jaws. When the rat presses down on the plate the jaws snap shut." Caput!

"I'll try it out " said Liam.

"I'll press down with my thumb".

"You'll never get it out in time" I warned him. We never thought of using a stick.

"I'll get it out alright, "Just watch".

The rat trap snapped shut and nearly severed his thumb. He lifted the trap with his other hand to take the weight off the wounded hand.

"I'll go home to my Mother", he grimaced.

We trooped in to his Mother. She took one look at his hand and nearly knocked us down as she raced past us. She left the front door wide open and ran in to my Mother next door. We followed slightly bemused unsure what to do. My Mother took control. She brought Liam in. Delicately she removed the trap. She washed his hand in very hot water and bathed the wound. Then she applied "Mercurochrome"- the wonder treatment of my childhood years. Amazingly there were only flesh wounds. She bandaged the hand. No doctor was consulted. No stitches were applied. It healed perfectly.

I thought about the rats and the traps and I dragged our expedition out as long as I could. I hoped by recounting the tale about the rats they would be as afraid of the rats, as I was, and that this might put them off. No such luck. We dawdled out along the tracks. There were all manner of distractions. We fired stones at the glazed cups on the telegraph poles that ran along the line. We searched for a yellow hammer's nest that we had located earlier. There were still no eggs in it. We had to pass the golf club which was beside the tracks. They could not be persuaded to search for golf balls that day. I hoped maybe my father would be about. No luck there either. I hoped the windows would be closed. No such luck. The back room faced north and was about three feet lower than the field at the back. To keep the room aired the top sash in the back bedroom window was propped by a lath to keep about three inches of it open.

Paddy was the tallest and the driving force behind our expedition. His left arm ended about two inches below his left elbow. He made light of his disability and could hold a sliothar in the crook of his elbow and he was a decent hurler. He later played on the Vocational Schools County Team and got a write up in the paper.

None of the rest of us was daring enough to try to open the window. Paddy had no such inhibitions. We could see the four rat traps around the hole in the floor. That did not slow him down. Slowly he prised the window open and climbed in. I tried to dissuade him. I said, "I'll be blamed."

"Your auld fellow will never find out. Anybody could have found the window open and climbed in", he replied

My stomach went through the proverbial floor. I was terrified. I felt as guilty as sin but there was no way out now. Paddy found a box of detonators and passed them out the window.

We scampered. The Northern Railway Line was just to the north of the field behind the cottage. A bohereen lead past the cottage up to and across the Northern Line. The boys admired the detonators and the simple yet ingenious way they could be attached to the rail.

We thought it safer to go out that line and away from town. It was one of the longest days of my life. My heart was in my mouth the whole time. Guilt was written all over my face.

Getting the detonators to "go off" was not easy. We tried hurling them at the rails and banging them with smallish stones but to no avail.

Paddy stumbled on the solution. He found a large rock and held it over his head with the two arms and banged the stone down on the detonator with all his might. It worked. The sight of him poised like Atlas over the rail with the rock grasped between the long and half arm is forever etched in my memory. He succeeded in exploding a few over a "long" afternoon. We were disappointed with the bangs.

As happens, small boys tire of every adventure so we turned for home. We had a good few detonators left. I was worried about leaving them where they could be found. Paddy had a solution. We had crossed a sizable river/stream on the outward journey. so we threw the detonators into the water where they could do no damage.

I was more relaxed on the way home. Relieved even. As we passed the end of the bohereen leading from the cottage I saw a flurry of movement from out of the long grass. Two men jumped out of hiding and apprehended us – my father and Tom, his able lieutenant.

"I'm in for it now" I thought. He quizzed us about the detonators. He knew we were guilty but how had he found out? He asked us our names even though he knew us all.

"Vincent Hussey Da" I mumbled when it came to my turn.

They marched us back out to the stream to recover the missing detonators. There was a rapid flow in the stream and the dreaded detonators had vanished.

We were released back at the top of the bohereen and we sloped back toward home. Suddenly all our legs were heavy and it was about 5.30 p.m. The fun was long gone even if there was never any in it for me. I had allowed myself to become an accomplice in crime and had no doubt that I would suffer as a result.

I was terrified when my father came home but he never mentioned anything at all about it. I kept a low profile!

I learned later that they had heard the detonators going off on the northern line. They knew that there was no gang working in that area on that day. There was no emergency that they knew of and there was nobody getting married. So they decided to investigate. They checked on the cottage, found the window open, the detonators missing and concluded correctly that they knew where the said detonators had gone! They suspected that children were involved as the window opening was not large. And that is how they captured us.

Anyone of us could have lost an ankle or a hand. We didn't realise how much danger we were in.

My father never mentioned the incident at `home.

Next day was my birthday. I figured that even though I had avoided a hiding that my birthday was bunched.

To my utter surprise my Mother brought me breakfast in bed next morning and an Annual "Boy's Own Companion". On the cover there was a coloured sketch of a group of fair haired footballers eating orange segments (then a luxury) at half time during a football match. It could have been a Gaelic match but on reading the book I found that it had to be a rugby match (then a banned game)! We were never offered anything at half time in any of the few matches that we played in.

Boy was I relieved and pleased. I still had that annual when I left home at eighteen years of age. I gave it to a younger cousin -but not anyone from Gallowsfields.

Vincent Hussey

"OFT, in the stilly night,
Ere slumber's chain has bound me,
Fond Memory brings the light
Of other days around me"
(Thomas Moore 1779-1852)

Saturday nights' "Fried TEA "

Evoke fond memory for me

Rashers and eggs deftly turned,

Pudding, sausages never burned.

"MOM" could rustle up the fry,

Without ever catching your eye,

Effortless it seemed to me

Her gentle soul infused the tea.

Love and Service in everything she did,

She never seemed to bat an eyelid.

Alas we took it all for granted

Nor showed the love she warranted.

She passed away one October,

All the boys showed up, sober,

Prayers were said, tears shed,

By the ones who most mourned.

She never asked for recompense,

It would last forever, was our sense,

Alas that could never be,

There's no one now for her "Fried TEA"

Vincent Hussey

OUR FIRST CAR

If we had known that it had twenty-five previous owners and had belonged to Jacky "Sull" we would never have bought it.

C.Mac and I paid £25 for it to BOD, a fellow engineering student. He said he would "help us to keep it on the road **".** He was brilliant and had a reputation for being "good with his hands. He married a girl that I indirectly introduced him to but sin scéal eile.

C.Mac was in final electrical while I was in final civil engineering. It was the autumn of 1966 and we had worked long hours in London during the summer.

It was the summer of Eusebio, Pele, Garrincha, Gordon Banks, Bobby and Jack Charlton, Martin Peters, Alan Ball, Geoff Hurst, Bobby Moore and Nobby Stiles. England won the 1966 world cup so all the natives were in good humour. We were in Millwall territory and they graciously told us that Charlie Hurley, an Irish player, was their best ever.

We worked thirteen twelve hour shifts every fortnight. We had just one 24 hour period "off" on the shift change over. We worked in one of the foulest smelling factories in Bermondsey making gelatine from animal bone. We stayed in a second floor bedsit in Deptford where we were the only Caucasians in the building. The house had a beautiful aroma of curry which was far more pleasant than the smell we brought back from the factory. It was in the heart of gangland, all the great train robbers, who were apprehended, came from within a four penny bus ride.

But back to Cork. We rented a two roomed flat in a respectable part of Sunday's Well. It was part of the landlady, Mrs O'B.s house. We had a large bedroom and a living room/kitchen. We used the landlady's front door. She was a lovely Motherly lady with two daughters who were nursing students in England. I think we occupied their former bedrooms. The house was located on a short dog-leg cul-de-sac off the Sunday's Well road. It stood on the bend of the dog-leg, behind a long front garden, and faced the main road. The frontage between it and the main road was dead in that it adjoined the deep back gardens of the larger houses on the Sundays' Well road.

We had accumulated enough money to last us for the year but we had a problem. We lodged our money in English Post Office savings books and we could only withdraw £10 at a time. To close the P.O. books and repatriate our money the books had to be transaction free for ten days. A feat we could not master. We found a solution.

A younger neighbour of mine J.C., who was a great basketball player, was starting in Fine Arts. He had worked in the German factory in Tralee since completing his Leaving Cert the previous June twelve months and saved enough money to go to college. His Mother only charged him £1 (one pound) a week for his keep. He had plenty of ready cash. We offered to take him in if he financed us long enough to retrieve our cash from England. He agreed.

Flush with cash we bought the Volkswagen. It had a working radio which was unusual at that time. It went o.k. but it had a defective exhaust and made a huge amount of noise which embarrassed our landlady. We lived up a hill on the cul-de-sac; we didn't start the engine until we got to the main road. It could also be parked discretely along a "dead" frontage at the entrance to the cul-de-sac so it didn't look as if it belonged to "our" house, small mercy!

Shortly after we moved in, Paudy K also from the Park, and like J.C., his father was a detective, needed a bed for six weeks. He was training to be a technician with the Dept. of Posts and Telegraphs and was doing a stint in the Crawford Technical College.

One weekend I had decided to go home to Tralee by train. I had subsidized travel on the trains because my father used to work on the railway. The boys decided to take the VW over the Cork and Kerry mountains to Tralee. I had serious reservations and didn't either trust them or the car.

They had just started on the Carrigrohane Straight out of Cork when the engine fell out of the car and landed on the roadway. Fortunately, at that time, the VW engine was located at the back of the car.

They were examining the wreckage when an unfortunate AA patrolman passed on his motorbike. They waved him down and joined on the spot. As Paudy K was the only one of them with a driver's licence they joined in his name. I had a driver's licence which I got when I was 17, before they introduced mandatory driving tests- foresight! But the other two had no licence. The AA towed the car back to a garage at Dennehy's Cross and the garage welded on a prop to restore the engine to its rightful place. The garage charged thirty shillings (30/-) for the repairs. So they made it across the mountain and back again. C. Mac fancied himself as a motor mechanic. I had no interest then, still have no interest in cars. He just had to meddle with the car. Oddly enough we never thought of getting the exhaust fixed to reduce the noise. We never thought of going to a garage to get it overhauled – guess we were too mean or too keen to do it ourselves. C max took out the cylinder head of the engine and the pistons out of the block. VW pistons are long and slender. In fairness to him the flat piston heads were pitted after twelve years of wear and tear. So we had most of the engine on a few newspapers in the corner of the living room and on the table a lot of the time. We sat down to grind the valves with paste. It is one tedious and time consuming job when done by hand. It involved dipping the piston head into the paste and spinning it backwards and forwards to wear the piston head to a new level. We didn't spill any oil on the floor but the smell of oil was forever in my nostrils... The car engine spent a long time on the floor. Then there were the "points" and the timing.

There was an incentive to get it back on the road again. In final year we each had to do a dissertation which had to be typed and bound. It would be unthinkable to have to pay to have the document typed. Typing was a skill in those days that could only be done by young ladies who worked in offices. I was lucky enough. In Civil three of us worked together on our dissertation. "The realignment of a Short Section of the Cork Bandon Road". We each had to contribute a couple of chapters. KOC "Cock" and J.M. shared with me. J.M. had worked with Cork Co. Co Roads department for the summer and took the precaution of persuading one of the young ladies in that office to type our report. C. Mac had to find a suitable young lady to type his. J.C. decided to help. So the VW was reassembled and the boys headed to Crosshaven to find a suitable candidate or candidates. Crosshaven was the "in" place at that time. It is a coastal resort about fifteen miles from Cork city and a well known boating centre. It was one of the few nights that I decided to stay home to study.

Not only did they find two young ladies who could and were willing to type his report but they were farmer's daughters from outside the city who fed us as well! They had a few drinks of course and were in high spirits. They broke the speed limits and crossed a white line. C.Mac was driving. They were overtaken by a Garda Car and waved down. They thought of running away but they couldn't really abandon the two young ladies. C.Mac rolled down the window and the Garda shone his torch in his face.

"Well, fuck you Mac" came the voice "and I needed a case". He was the only Garda in Cork city that C.Mac knew. He was from his home place. The only document they had with them was my driver's licence so I was always at risk of picking up a summons for some misdemeanour or worse.

They arrived back to the flat with the two young ladies in tow. J.C. entered the room cautiously. I was sitting behind the door. Then a very sheepish C.Mac came in and waved to the two young ladies who came in tentatively. One of them had blonde hair and looked strangely at me. I was my usual welcoming self and offered to make tea! Much later they told me that they had told the blonde lady that their flatmate reacted violently to blondes and that they would check first to see if I was calm and if it was safe for her to venture in! As I say they were lovely girls and often brought the two out home to feed them. J.C. had no shame but C.Mac had a sense of decorum and would not gorge himself.

Paudy K left for the next part of his training and left a black polo neck top behind. J.C. wore it during the day and C.Mac wore it in bed. By Christmas it could stand up by itself. J.C. brought it home with him. His Mother washed it and it lost a proverbial stone weight. The VW came back to Tralee too for Christmas. It was down around the "Park" and some neighbour complained about the noise. As J.C. was a detective's son it remained parked so as not to embarrass his father. It did however return to Cork – but not for long.

It stopped up near the north Cathedral with C.Mac driving. So he left it. He decided that the fuel injector was not working so he tried to bypass it using a rubber hose that he "borrowed" from the lab. The two of us went up next day to retrieve the car. He disconnected the fuel pipe which had a narrow gauge and replaced it with the much larger rubber hose and then tried to siphon the petrol from the petrol tank to the engine. He very nearly got sick from inhaling the fumes. We eventually got it going but it never went properly again. There was a vehicle dismantler on the outskirts of the city who offered to buy the car for £10 (ten pounds for the radio he said) but the boys felt they could do better.

They put an ad, under my name, in the Cork Evening Echo together with the landlady's phone number. "VW car parts for sale". Well the phone was hopping! After the first few calls I saw the boys slipping off out the front gate leaving me to face the landlady! I told anyone else who got through that everything was sold. The landlady understood that I was the fall guy. I did all our dealings with her, paid the rent and so on.

We ate humble pie and sold the VW for the £10 (ten pounds) and were glad to be rid of it. Meanwhile K.O'C had brought a Daimler back from England with him. There were probably only a handful of Daimlers in the country. They were a luxury car, with leather upholstery and could seat eight comfortably. It surely had an array of eight lights on the front.

The problem was he didn't have a registration book for it and needed another £50 (fifty pounds) to get the "wide boy" he bought it from to part with the papers. He didn't have £50 (fifty pounds). He came to C.Mac and me to pay the balance. We couldn't trust the deal so we wouldn't cough up. Anyway we had the VW. One evening around dusk he was cruising on park lights only when a Garda stopped him One of the park lights was not working. He asked to see the tax and insurance for the car which could not be produced. He gave him the usual ten days to produce them to a local garda station.

C.Mac asked his friendly Garda to intervene. The other Garda would not relent and would agree not to press charges only if the car was taken off the road.

So the Daimler was parked in a cul-de-sac on the Southside of the city. It was stripped of anything that was removable in a matter of days. K.O'C had to pay the City corporation thirty shillings (30/-) to remove it to a scrap yard.

"Once bitten, twice shy". Not a bit of it. "Hope springs eternal". Next we bought a Renault Dauphine again from B.O'D for £30 (thirty pounds) – a move upmarket. It had only three forward gears and again it didn't have the power of the VW. So guess what? C.Mac had to take it apart again. This time it did several tours of duty on our living room floor and table before being put back together again. There were two added complications! First it was a French car and sizes were metric. We were still using imperial measurements in this part of the world. There was one spanner that was essential to remount the engine. It could not be got in Cork. Luckily the AA inspector drove a Renault Dauphine and owned the appropriate spanner. So we would call up the AA when we needed to remount the engine and ask for their help. We regularly had four AA men peering into the void left by the engine. One of the two boys, I usually did not attend the ceremonies, would suggest politely that the Inspector knew what to do i.e. he had the correct spanner. So the conversation would go something like

"Number One, Number four here, I'm attending a break down in Sunday's Well. It's a Renault Dauphine and you have special expertise with this car as you drive one yourself."

So we had the Inspector as well as everybody else.

Number two in Cork city was Dinny Riley from Kilorglin and he was Chairman of the Co. Kerry Basketball Board. He knew J.C and myself and got to know the others. One time when he turned out in response to our call he asked

"Which one of you guys is Paudy K this time?"

The two lads got embarrassed so they sent me out the next time. The car was in its usual resting place beside the dead frontage with the engine hanging out.

"The engine kind of fell out when we were trying to start it" I mumbled feeling very foolish, conscious of the two boys above leering out the front window.

Fortunately, that AA man knew the routine and so didn't need to be prompted to call No 1.

Worse was to come. C.Mac decided to remove the cylinder head. Unfortunately the cylinder head gasket which was made of a cork like cardboard, crumbled. He bought a sheet of gasket paper and told me, as the Civil Engineer, to cut out a new gasket. The gasket paper was flat while the Renault gasket had to negotiate a mound in the engine housing; I couldn't bend the gasket paper. I had to introduce a joint into it and I had no way of fusing the two ends together. When the engine was turned on oil spewed out through the joint. We rigged up an oil tin, suspended from a wire clothes hanger under the leak to collect the oil which we then periodically emptied back into the engine.

Whenever somebody reversed into a kerb the oil spilled so we left many oil slicks on the kerbs around Sunday's well and other places.

Around then an oil tanker by the name of "Torrey Canyon" ran aground in the English Channel and discharged two hundred thousand tons of crude oil into the sea. It caused thousands of fish and bird kills and did huge environmental damage. At one time the RAF bombed the oil slick to try to cause it to break up or to burn it off. They had no real success. Miles of coast had to be painstakingly cleared of oil slicks. I christened the Dauphine the "Torrey Canyon". The pictures of sea birds with their plumage covered in oil were heart rending on T.V. As luck would have it, there was a large house down the road from us where several Gardai, stationed in Sundays Well, shared accommodation with one of my class mates. We got several warnings about our vehicle and eventually it came to the attention of their Sergeant who had been a well known Cork footballer. He insisted that the Torrey Canyon had to go.

It was notoriously unreliable. We gave one of our mates, who lived nearby, a lift to college one morning – we weren't on time that often. Walking we could use the pedestrian suspension bridge over the Lee and the walk was fairly manageable. By road it was much further. Of course the car broke down and he had to help us to push it a far greater distance. We kept him late. He never again accepted a lift from us and blackened our reputation.

I was captain of the college basketball team and JC and myself had a game every Wednesday night in the hall in Gurranabraher, which was on top of one of the many hills in Cork, and basically uphill of Sunday's Well and Blarney Street. One night C.Mac was going to a dance in college (in the Rest). We were under strict orders to have the car back in time so he could drive. On his way in, the car ran out of petrol on the Western Road and he had to push it on his own for about two hundred yards to a petrol station. He got sick with the physical effort. We got some abuse over that incident. Exams and summer was fast approaching. In final year they employed a Consultant Engineer who had returned from Canada to "teach" us design. He set up classes on Wednesday nights which clashed with our basketball matches. I didn't get to go to his classes until the basketball season ended. We had a really good team that year – five from Kerry and a couple from Cork. We actually won the intervarsity – Scott McLed Cup, beating Trinity in the final.

The 1967 Arab-Israeli war was another huge distraction. C.Mac and I were very much pro-Israeli. They seemed to be totally outnumbered and outgunned but won hands down largely because they had U.S. backing and equipment.

So exams over, we breathed a sigh of relief and began to celebrate. The faculty even brought us to dinner in the Cork Boat Club. We had to pay for the dinner but C.Mac and I both qualified – Phew!

Nobody wanted the Renault. We couldn't sell it in its condition. So we parked it down in "Lee Fields" beside that famous river. In no time at all it was stripped. Even the engine block was removed. So the Corporation was called in again and we parted with another 30/-(thirty shillings).

Vincent Hussey

Acknowledgements

Without the active support and encouragement of my wife Pauline and our five grown-up children I would not be writing.

I would not be this far down the road without Pauline McNamee and her creative writing workshops. She provided inspiration to all of us who participated in them. As I always say she gave us permission to write "badly" but to write.

The Staff of Tullamore Branch Library have provided a magnificent resource. Their unfailing good humour and willingness to provide facilities and help is vital and just brilliant.

Finally, I wish to acknowledge the support and encouragement provided by my fellow Wordsmiths. They are an extraordinary group of writers. I am in awe of their skills and talents. Their support is immeasurable.

There is literally never "a discouraging word".

To all the foregoing I extend my sincere thanks.

MARY CULLOTY

Morning Breakfast

An Ode To My Sick Day

Me-Fein-A-Dhein E

I Made Him

Biography

Mary, born in Tullamore, growing up in the vibrant town enriched her experiences of life and the wild joys in living. An author, home-maker, proud wife and Mother to Eugene and Jack, Mary's interests include creative writing, poetry, monologues and short stories.

Mary cared for her beautiful Mother, Tess, until she recently acquired her wings. Mary now has a philosophy ***"Today's tragic/terrible experience will become tomorrow's funny story"*** and because of her life experiences Mary knows the value of love and the importance of gratitude with these gifts her life has become more entertaining. Mary's dream is to continue to swim in creative waters.

Morning Breakfast

"What's that clattering in the kitchen? With any luck a FRY.

I hope he's not doing it, everything will be fried to just an inch of its life. Can't understand it? Why! does he not think of the washing up after his culinary exploits or understand it? NOOOOO! Let *him* try and WASH was a frying pan that's been used to char food put on it.

Yeeeeep! It's him, listen to the loud sizzling of ....

..... ooooh I hope sausages and not the rashers, nothing is as bad as frying things in the wrong order,

...... going down on the hot oil, can't understand why they don't use dripping, just the flavour alone, what can I say! A pound to a penny part of the sausage will be scorched.

The mushrooms, I wonder if they are on and in a saucepan, cooking in plenty of butter and not the muck they now call "spread". Spread me eye, it's glorified margarine, half butter (I don't think!) and oil. Maybe I should shout down to him not to put salt in until the end of cooking and remind him what happened the last time! He cooked mushrooms, they were as dry as the skin of a rhino or is it a hippo? oh it doesn't matter, 'cause the salt takes all the moisture out, but does he listen!, well we'll see.

I know he thinks I'm a cantankerous old *BAT* but I'mmmm*only* starting, he hasn't seen anything yet and, ah! he's a big by and sure I (cough) him.

Anyway, wonder if he's putting on, ohh what do you call those things, those triangular yokes that the American's go mad for, I told him before and I'll tell him again I DON'T LIKE THEM, they're a soggy lump of mush and no one can tell me they are lovely 'cause THEY ARE NOT.

Oh, I hope there's pudding on the plate, like both of them, black or white, but to be truthful I'd prefer the white, (laughing) there'll be some stink in the room before the day is out, some of the stories I've heard, well, ahahahaha.

Beans, love them but they don't love me and on top of the pudding that I might eat God there'll be not air in the room after I'm finished, PEEEWWWW, and anyway really I don't want them especially if they touch my egg, better be a DUCK, you have to have the taste and those chickens don't do it for me, you need a nice orange, runny yoke mmmmm, can you just mmmmm!

Now that I think of it, didn't smell any brown bread cooking yesterday, hope she made some, a fry is not a fry unless you have homemade brown bread, that stuff you get in some of the shop, well don't get me started on that or we'll be here until tomorrow and, even if I say so myself, she does a good bread, eh! would never tell her that but she gets it from me, and anyway if they'd let me I'd cook, YES I'd cook really yeah really I would.

Someone's on their way, oh I can just taste the buttery mushrooms, crispy rashers, sausages, pudding, egg and hopefully tomato with brown bread and a lovely cup of tea.

WHAT THE HELL IS THIS?

PORRIDGE!!!!!!!!!!!"

Mary Culloty

An Ode To My Sick Day

Oh, to have the sympathy of others on the day

that I be ill

But for me useless empathy from those

who do not know

I have a head that now believes a drum kit now resides

A nose that runs a watery sprint and then it hits

the wall

That blocks the air passage at the bridge

just between my two eyes

That now have heavy lids which really do not

want to rise

My pupils straining painfully against the

streaming light

And not to mention my poor teeth that ache

Oh, my poor brain now wishing they be dentures

so I could take them out

But no sympathy for me as for all I hear is

"That is nothing 'cause when I had..."

No stop! I really don't want to know 'cause at

This time I don't care if you or

Anyone else have or had what’s maybe ailing me

Tomorrow I may feel better but just for today

allow me to be ill, so please just

Love me and pity me and let me wallow through

my sick day

Mary Culloty

Mé Féin A Dhein É

M'faire do ar mo Cuisle
Le grá, buiochas gáirim l'athais
MÉ FÉIN A DHEIN É

Is gan dearmad ar an síol a chbraigh liom
Is Cuma mar
MÉ FÉIN A DHEIN É

Feachaim ar a chumas, comh laidir is comh lag
Agus tá mé lán sásta liom féin
MÉ FÉ IN A SHEIN É

Breathnaím ar na súla geala, grásta, grámhar
A cruthú gor liomsa thú
Is chomh móralach atá mé
MÉ FÉIN A DHEIN É

Fairim fás imeallach cnamha is craiceann
Agus tá lúchair orm
MÉ FÉIN A DHEIN É

Cloisim an gaire, an fulaingt, an aoibhneas
An sult a thugann sé do cách agus
Glaoim ós árd
MÉ FÉIN A DEIN É

Cím an agaidh, mion gáire, an gealán agus
Gaisce mo bhuachall bhán agus soilsigh
MÉ FÉIN A DHEIN É

Ach sé Neart mo corp, fuinneamh m'anam a thug

Go dtí an domhain seo

M'BUACHALL M'STÓR

Go raibh maith agat go mór as do chabhair Vincent Hussey

Mary Culloty

I Made Him

I look upon my child and revel with joy and love and exclaim

I Made Him

For not forgetting the sperm that helped, it doesn't matter for

I Made Him

I look upon the structure, so strong and yet so frail and

Bask in the knowledge of

I Made Him

I view the eyes that shine of grace and love that makes you mine and I'm so proud that

I Made Him

I watch the outer growth of bones and skin and rejoice in the fact that

I Made Him

I hear the laughter, the pain, the joy, the fun he brings to all and I shout

I Made Him

I see the face, the smile, the sparkle and the actions of my cherished boy and I glen

I Made Him

Oh the power of my body, the energy of my soul that brought to this world

My Precious Boy

Mary Culloty

Acknowledgements

To my Mother for her spiritual inspiration.

To the Tullamore Wordsmiths, with their support and motivating spirit I have been able to allow myself to write my own words.

And my family for listening to what seems to start as ravings and develops into what I can put on paper.

MARY CAMPBELL

Mary Campbell - Bio

Coming from a large family of artistic types always trying to out-best each other at home, Mary always had a team of critics around to keep her feet firmly on the ground. Her songs and poems came up against stiff competition from sibling writers, artists and musicians (all amateur and self-professed!). Growing up in humble surroundings and with so much talent in the family she never imagined she could make a career as a writer or poet. Down the years she has drawn on her talent for creativity to write amateur plays and musicals for community groups and children, while every single wedding card she gifted contained beautifully worded personalised poetry. It is only in recent years that she started writing in earnest and writing as a hobby became a form of therapy to guide her through tough times and she rediscovered her passion. She has written her first book which has gone out to agents and publishing houses and she is currently working on another, determined at last to make a career as an author.

She couldn't have done any of this without the wonderful encouragement and support of the Tullamore Wordsmiths, who have become family to her. It is because of them that she has finally stepped out of the shadows and is ready to share her poetry and writing with the world. Her favourite tag line is "Tread softly because you tread on my dreams" from her favourite poet WB Yeats, so please tread softly when reading her work, because it is the stuff of her dreams!

Anti-Social

Sitting in your halo of morning sunshine

Streaming gloriously through double glass doors

My sweet boy, desperately seeking friendship

Dejected, unemployed, and feeling poor

Unseeing of red breasted Robin begging

Nor snow blanket sparkling on the step outside

Phone in hand scrolling through other's stories

Lustful, full of envy, for other's lives

Smiling happy selfies, exotic destinations,

Prizes to be won, just share and like

At what point did you archive reality?

Disconnect the power source from your life

I'm witnessing a new world wide epidemic

A man made virus more crippling than 'er seen

Your world around you is slowly shrinking

Into cleverly airbrushed images on your screen

I once saw in you such talent and potential

Imagined the successful happy man you'd become

Instead I grow ever more fearful

Social media is destroying you my son

You who once thrilled to brave a rain storm

Swimming in choppy freezing cold seas

I curse the day that you swiped left

Deleting all of your spirit and childhood dreams

Tell me what's smart about these smart phones?

Hypnotised to like a stranger's page

My boy who once downloaded real adventure

Willingly climbs into an imaginary gilded cage

For cages are exactly what they build for him

Fake digital platforms, wherein he lives

Timed out from this beautiful world around him

From sensory experiences that no App can give

You cannot smell a pixelated blossom

Feel stock images of wet sand between your toes

Nor can any shiny Otterbox protect you

From growing old and actual real time woes

Popularity, is naught but a clever cyber hoax

Five hundred friends, each with a glowing daily post

But no letters drop through your mail box

No warm hugs, no someone special to hold

The only kisses that you get are xxx's

No *one on one* on the basketball court

Only sharing viral uTube videos or photos

Allowing strangers' comments to cause you hurt

What is the deal with this new text speak

Emojis crying to explain when you're feeling low

But still no one comes a knocking

And online isn't a real place to go

Streams with no thirst quenching water

Filtered news not on paper but blogs

Only reading 'bout stuff that is trending

Broken marriages, celebrities lives on the rocks

Could I as a Mother have stopped this?

Kept you away from the anonymous Trolls

Influenced your childhood with more tough love

Insisted on instilling in you more concrete goals?

Please wake up to this anti-social media

Jump on and experience the roller coaster ride

Plug back into non Virtual Reality

When you do, you'll see, it's a wonderful life!

Mary Campbell

SAND DUNES

Danger 'neath the overhang

Worn paths

In erratic pattern

Half hidden by Marram grass

Slippery slope

Treacherous

Not to surefooted goat

Just us

Fun seekers

Barefooted

Freed from sneakers

Escapees

Sharp sea breeze

Leaves us blind

Blowing sand and debris

To slow our climb

Squeals of delight

Skidding out of sight

But oh the adventure

As we slip and slide

Down to the beach

To meet the tide.

Mary Campbell

The ABC guide to True Happiness

Acceptance of who you are, is the first step you'll agree

Before you can find true happiness, be what you can be

Communicate your true feelings, try open up your heart

Dump your negativity, be positive from the start

Enjoy the open air around you, get some exercise

Find the beauty in the simple things, nature never lies

Give thanks and praise to God each day, and try to love yourself

Help if support is needed, but accept when you need help

Invest yourself in new subjects, 'tis never a bad thing

Journey your mind to distant realms, the mysteries they bring

Knowledge gives you real power, to overcome all your fears

Learn how to be a better you, don't imitate your peers

Motivate others to follow you, good things that you do

Never envy other people, to your own self be true

Open your mind to opportunities, try taking a risk

Push yourself to new limits, regret not what you have missed

Question all those in authority, don't stay in the dark

Recognise fact not fiction, the truth will take you far

Socialise only with good folk, become a better friend

Try being ever trustworthy, broken trust is hard to mend

Understand we all have flaws, forgive others when you can

Value truth and loyalty, but try not to reprimand

Words can cut deeper than knives, do not make anyone cry

X's are not real kisses, eye contact won't ever lie

You must try to engage with people, go and share some fun

Zestfully try all of these and true happiness will come

Mary Campbell

Still Me

These eyes of mine no longer sparkle

I look out through cataract misted lens

The portholes once firm and unwrinkled

Azure blue diamonds, once the envy of my friends

But I myself still reside here

The view from my seat still the same

My thoughts and my dreams, they are ageless

I still go by the very same name.

Mary Campbell

Blast from the Past

I look in the mirror, and what do I see?

A blast from the past, and that blast is me

Surprised but happy to see a familiar face

Glad I am finally, leaving that dark place

The eyes that look back at me, sparkle with hope

Dull grey skin vanished, cheeks tinted rose

For a while I was missing, my soul was dead

I had lost my identity, nearly lost my head

Weighed down by life's rejections, I was lost

A shadow of my former self, merely a ghost

But I have my MOJO back, I'm writing again

The old I is emerging, on the back of my pen

I've a new lease of life; I am ready to fight

Much happier and stronger now, embracing my life

Mary Campbell

Golden Moments

As evening falls

Wandering barefoot by the coast

Benbulben's shadow calls

To me, fellow lonesome ghost

Perched high amid the sand dunes

I too, sit and wait

Basking in sun's fiery plumes

Before it gets too late

Eyes closed, I breathe

Peace enfolds me like a cloak

With nought but salty breeze

And hissing song of ebb and flow

Of sleepy waves, reduced to trickle,

In crawling token roll

Sharp Marram underfoot, but a tickle

Between my sandy toes

Shivering, I chafe my cooling skin

As she dips her skirts into the sea

Her warm golden kiss

Bids good night to me.

Mary Campbell

The Cave

In the darkest recesses of my mind, a covert haunt I call the cave

No mortal man may enter there, lest he too become enslaved

I guard the entrance warily, keeping stealthy pirates out

Their wily ways won't get them in, gold Doubloons hold little clout

Memories like skeletons buried deep, imprisoned in murky gloom

For fear the dead will walk again, awaken far too soon

In chains, tortured far too long, at last I mutinied their ship

Relegated them like detritus, to dank and mouldy skip

Like buccaneer up Jacob's ladder, with cutlass in my hand

I scuttled that shadowy man o' war, swam back to dry land

It took a tidal wave of bravery to overcome their swords

Cast them in the mouth of hell, silencing their damning words

I rose above the murky depths, avoided drowning in despair

My youthful faith it carried me, when none around did care

The stout walls of my cave will hold, as long as I stand strong

Leaving secret thoughts to rot, where they can do no wrong

I'll not revisit that dark place, wherein haunts my slimy ghouls

The next time I may not escape, might no longer have the tools

I smell the stench from time to time, the rank odour of decay

Then crawl back off the slippery dock, to keep the sharks at bay

If I could I'd banish them forever, into a cold and watery grave

For tide it turns, can't be deterred, and I remain shackled to that cave

Mary Campbell

Planet Lost

Fishing plastics from our oceans
Was never in God's plan
We should eat the brooks resources
Never build a dam

We were meant to share with others
Not throw away our food
Or burn our unsold produce
While the homeless root

We should be plucking from nature
Her balms and her cures
Using time honoured remedies
Avoiding pharmaceutical lures
Our landfills are growing bigger
As consumerism soars
Leaching chemicals into our rivers
From which our water pours

Rain forests that replenish our air
Are slain for paper cups
Soon discarded everywhere
To sate our coffee lust

Industries emit harmful gasses

To create a better world?

Building luxury goods for the masses

While whole mountains of forestry burn

Slaves to take away fast food

Over processed, over cheap

Pumping poisons into our children's blood

Putting farmers on the scrap heap

Climate change alone won't kills us

But materialism will

Fuelling more poverty and abuse

Ingesting chemicals that kill

We need to go back to our roots

And help our planet heal and grow

For when it dies, it's us who'll lose

We will reap what we sow!

Mary Campbell

Cold Heart

Just as winter looms

So creep you

Like stealthy snow clouds

Dark and forbidding

Bringing decay

Destruction

And I set adrift

Barren and windswept

After the storm

Nought left

But stark and lonely silhouette

On slippery stage,

Shivering

Cowering against the cold

Up there alone

Frozen

Under arctic gaze

That pierces my skull

Your icy stare

Stems my flow

Yet you linger

Lurking in the shadows

Where you thrive

With evil intent

Silently directing the scene

Like cold hand at my back

A cutting breeze

Chilling my bones

Razor sharp words

Like icy fingers

Squeezing the breath from me

Ill-timed prompts

Like poison in my ear

Or a sheet of hail

Your contempt

With frosty bite

Like icy daggers

Hidden from sight

Or a black frost

Treacherous underfoot

Once swept off my feet

Now tripped!

Mary Campbell

Closing time

When the sun sets and curtains close
Companionable silence ensues
All's left between us memories
Dying embers to warm our toes

Lamp light dimmed, in cosy glow
Snuggled up 'neath threadbare rug
Peace broken only by occasional snore
Arthritic hands rattling the jug

A weak cup of tea for a night cap
No more whiskey, no more wine
No more frisky, fondling under covers
No more dreaming, no more time

Yet we do not miss those things
No longer need to watch the clock
We don't worry what the night may bring
Or that we've almost reached our stop
Content we've had our day in the sun
Hand in hand watched that sun go down
Our only wish, to raise a glass together
When closing time comes around

Mary Campbell

Cold Heart

Just as winter looms

So creep you

Like stealthy snow clouds

Dark and forbidding

Bringing decay

Destruction

And I set adrift

Barren and windswept

After the storm

Nought left

But stark and lonely silhouette

On slippery stage,

Shivering

Cowering against the cold

Up there alone

Frozen

Under arctic gaze

That pierces my skull

Your icy stare

Stems my flow

Yet you linger

Lurking in the shadows

Where you thrive

With evil intent

Silently directing the scene

Like cold hand at my back

A cutting breeze

Chilling my bones

Razor sharp words

Like icy fingers

Squeezing the breath from me

Ill-timed prompts

Like poison in my ear

Or a sheet of hail

Your contempt

With frosty bite

Like icy daggers

Hidden from sight

Or a black frost

Treacherous underfoot

Once swept off my feet

Now tripped

Mary Campbell

From the Ashes

From the ashes of disaster
Female kind have risen up
Trusting eyes have been opened
We'll n'er more drink from poisoned cup

The church in silence hides from us
Redress will not freely come
But evil soon will be vanquished
Our freedom will see the sun

If women stand strong together
Of one righteous united mind
Our collective voices will be louder
We will break these ties that bind

Our skills and talent long suppressed
Wounded men's egos to defend
T'was but a childish power struggle
Of much weaker minded men

Soon the tides of change will turn
Change for this world's greater good
Equality and fairness will be re-planted
Where once bigotry and evil stood

Mary Campbell

I am worth more than someone's second choice

No longer someone's back up plan, I ran

Unwilling to settle for second place

How can I be no one without a man?

Why let that lie be shoved into my face?

Free at last among new supportive friends

Who raised my self-esteem and gave me wings

Assured me that's not how my story ends

Pushed me on to bigger and better things

With confidence I learned to use my voice

To ask for what I want and not sit back

I am worth more than someone's second choice

Capable to walk a different track

Though I still have such a long way to go

I'll resurrect the girl I used to know

Mary Campbell

June Blues

Grey summer morning

Hot cup of tea in hand

Light rain still falling

I gaze out 'cross sodden land

No cheery birds on song

Sheltering mid the leaves

They gaze out where they belong

Floating high upon a breeze

Melancholy I too feel

Tis late June after all

Warm sunshine was the deal

Not wet and windy squall

Reflecting mood within

Children out of sorts

Nary a chance to swim

Marshy ground unfit for sports

And oh what damp chill

Tis colder now than spring

And I with time to kill

Ponder what July will bring

Mary Campbell

Reverse

Sliding backwards

Undoing

Eradicating

Years of struggle

Lives lost

And given

To the cause

Of just

And humanity

This greed

And lust

To earn a crust

Cheapen our labour

Corners cut

To benefit the few

While others slave

In sweatshops

To the grave

No thought for age

Or rights

Or needs or wants

But ours

And while we eat

Others weep

And die

In Trumped up wars

Fuelled by hate

And oft

The need to prop

Jobs

Work for soldiers

Engineers

Munitions makers

Profiteers

Like Vultures

Empowered

Aided and abetted

By the state

Banks cossetted

Landlords safe

Rents raised

Homes repossessed

Families dispossessed

Celtic Tiger slain

No moving forward

No progress

In reverse

Fallen from the wagon

We digress

Clock rewound

Not survival of the fittest

Survival of the few

It could be you

Mary Campbell

Tainted

Forgive him not, our wasted tears

On one who pillaged, lives destroyed

Fools we mourned him, all these years

Rehashing memories to fill the void

A disgraced hero, dragged from his pedestal

The Fairy-tale splintered like Camelot

Out from the woodwork, his sins expelled

Bruised victims would not be forgot

Oh how he mocks us now from the grave

Rose tinted lens, at long last removed

Cheated, we uncover all he betrayed

A legacy of deceit, from one so beloved

How could we not see through his veneer

'neath the surface a deviant nature lurked

And now as the dust starts to clear

We lament all the innocents he hurt

The condolences book has been shut

We'll bury our memories with him in the ground

Good riddance, at last banished underfoot

Bon voyage to hell, o two faced clown!

Mary Campbell

The Long Finger Folly

Time's stolen, by procrastination

Long fingers, should only hold rings

A problem's never solved by deferral

Fear seldom conquered, by hiding

Dare not, put off till tomorrow or later

What you can, in all honesty, do today

Beware, what opportunities are oftmissed

When you drag your feet, when you delay

To postpone, is to risk never doing

For who knows what tomorrow may bring

An open door, may not long stay open

Broken promises, oft carry a sting

So be true to your word, when you give it

Carry through, and don't ever be late

Dream of a better life, and then live it!

For you forfeit all, when you procrastinate

Mary Campbell

Trapped

Behind closed doors

Picture and no sound, deafening silence

The power firmly in his hands, his purse strings

His house, his car, his family his voice

Not mine, I open my mouth but no words come

Frantic, trying to escape but in my head only

Tears, under covers unheard in the dark

On the edge, sleeping with one eye shut

Exhausted, no sound, yet inside I'm screaming

No work, application follows application, but nothing

Don't they know? I need this, desperately need to get out

But no, not even a rejection letter, just silence

Watching, but the postman doesn't come, nothing for me

Waiting, too quiet in the house, I jump at every noise

Alone, just battling my thoughts, then schools out

Chaos, like a whirlwind they thrash about

Breaking the peace, but the distraction is welcome

So happy, unknowing, but tis better this way

Ignorant bliss, for them nothing seems to change

Thankful, I count the years till they're gone

Safe, far away, from this farcical fiction he constructs

I'll leave then, job or not I'll find something to do

Anything, nothing can be worse than this inertia,

this pain, yet I continue painting on the mammy smile

No bruises, just completely beaten, a broken heart

and mind, somehow its worse with nothing to show

No visible scars, just profound unhappiness and fear

No life, but if he went what would we do?

If I go, what then, what's next?

Cannot stay, yet cannot go

Trapped

Mary Campbell

Acknowledgements

To all the people who've crossed my path and made an impact on my life, whether good or bad, I salute you. Without the highs and the lows and the rollercoaster ride that has been my life thus far, I would never have had so much material to draw on for my writing. While I have not defamed or characterized any of you unkindly in my writing there are facets of all my life experiences and those of people around me contained in these pages, and which I used to inspire the emotional and often dark stories contained in my verses. I am grateful for a very colourful childhood and the boundless love of my extraordinary parents who, while far from saints, have always been supportive of all of our dreams. We came from nothing but were always told we could be anything we wanted to be and that is worth more to me than all the riches in the world. I have a great family and some really special friends who keep my head above water and push me to be a better me. I thank you all from the bottom of my heart, but my greatest gratitude must be allocated to the wonderful team of Wordsmiths Tullamore who buoy me up every week with words of encouragement and give me the confidence to come out of the closet. This is me! Like it or loathe it, all the words are mine and I thank you for taking the time to share this journey with me.

PAUL HOLMES

The Thought Bubble

Impact

Biography

Paul Holmes is a Tullamore native. After working in Finance for a number of years in Dublin, he returned to college and gained qualifications in Information Technology and teaching English. In 2014 he was proclaimed 'Master of Fine Arts in Creative Writing' by American College Dublin, graduating with first class honours. He has hosted writers' workshops and his writing focus is on short stories and novels. He also has an interest in scriptwriting.

The Thought Bubble

I'm standing on Nassau Street leaning against the grey stone wall that surrounds Trinity College waiting for my bus to arrive. It's that time in the evening when everyone is heading home, so there are plenty of people around, many like myself waiting for transportation, others moving hurriedly through the passages created between the crowds of people situated on either side of the footpath, those by the kerb queuing to board while those on the inside waiting for an arrival. I look over to the real time information display to check what time my bus will appear and leaning just in front of the metal post for the display is a man. Just a normal guy, white trainers on, jeans and a jacket, scarf and a beanie hat, slim, clean shaven, nothing really remarkable about him. As he's standing there this little circle, about the size of a saucer just appears out of thin air above his head. It's chalk white and surrounded by a black outline. I'm stunned and I just stand there, mouth open in shock staring at the guy. He doesn't seem to notice that it's there and I look about the crowd, but by the lack of reaction I discern that no one else seems to notice it either. I look back at the guy and now there are two circles, the saucer sized one and another twice its size hovering to the right above it. As I'm staring in disbelief one more appears, double the size again. They're all chalk white and have the black outline surrounding them.

One more appears. It has the same chalk white colour with black outline but it is much bigger than the others and is oval in shape. It's directly above his head and blocking out the bus times. I start to think I'm going mad. Losing the plot. Maybe someone slipped something into my coffee earlier. I'm frantically looking around and everyone else on the street seems oblivious to this. I rub my eyes, look again and they are still there and then the oval begins to ripple like a pond when a stone is thrown in and colours spread out from its centre and blurred images start to appear. A series of different images flash up hurriedly and I'm only catching one or two visions as they present hazy. One is a group of people in an office, another of books on a shelf and another of a goal being scored during a football game and they speed up so much that it's just a blur, no single image registers with me as they are moving so quickly and then they just come to a dead stop and the oval returns to chalk white. I'm really starting to panic now, my breathing is shallow and quick and my heart is beating heavy in my chest. What the hell is happening to me?

In the oval now an image of a young woman appears and it's clear as day, much clearer than the previous ones. She's very pretty, is wearing glasses and has blonde shoulder length hair with a fringe that's swept off to the right joining in with the rest of the golden locks. She's talking on the phone and smiling a genuine smile where her eyes light up and her face is beaming. I'm looking at this image and for the first time I notice the background in it and I see the long grey stone wall, the one I'm standing beside and I turn to look down the street and there she is walking in our direction. The pretty girl is on the footpath walking through the channel of commuters and the guy is looking at her and she's on view in the image above his head, his eyes are a camera recording the images in front of him and the oval is the display. I'm looking back and forth between the two, she's talking and smiling and walking towards us and the image above the man's head starts to change. She's still a good one hundred metres away, but in the oval she is walking past him and her phone slips from her hand and he catches it in mid-air. He smiles as he's handing it back to her and their hands touch for a brief moment, their eyes are locked on one another, both smiling now and completely engaged.

Images of them together appear in the oval. First they are standing in a town square before a large Christmas tree. People are walking around with shopping bags and the lights on the tree come on. He places his left hand on her cheek and leans in and kisses her.

Then they are in a room with no furniture and there are boxes everywhere. Blue paint is sprinkled on their clothes, trays, brushes and rollers sit on a tarp on the ground, the walls half finished. They are sitting on the floor by an open fire, eating takeout, talking and drinking wine.

Then she's wearing a white dress and he is placing a ring on her finger as vows are said in front of a priest, both of them with a smile on their face and surrounded by friends and family.

He lays a new-born child into a bassinet as she watches on from the doorway of a nursery that has trees and animals painted on the walls.

Then in a garden, and there are lots of children of various ages and sizes, girls and boys, running around throwing water balloons at one another as the sun shines down on all of them.

Now they are much older and standing by a hospital bed. A young woman who has some features of both of them is holding a new-born, his arm is over her shoulder and they are both beaming with joy, and suddenly the images stop and just the chalk white backdrop remains.

I look at his face and his eyes are darting back and forth moving from the ground and back to the girl. She walks past me laughing into her phone and is only a couple of paces away from him. He looks up to her and in anticipation he takes his right hand out of his jacket pocket and straightens up, the oval now blank above his head, his attention on her completely.

And she walks past him. Just walked right by, chatting and giggling into the phone that's still secure in her hand and his gaze shifts to the ground. I look at her again and she is walking on down the footpath getting lost in the crowd. I turn back to him, standing at the bus stop, white trainers on, jeans and jacket, scarf and hat, his hands in his pockets, chin on his chest, jaw tense and a blank stare towards the ground, but in the chalk white oval above his head surrounded by a black outline is an image of himself, hiding his eyes behind his left hand and shaking his head slowly back and forth. His right hand is hanging by his side and it balls up into a fist and strikes the pole behind him once, twice and then three times in quick succession. He takes a deep breath and lets out a roar, before sliding his back down the pole bringing his chest to his knees and burying his face into his hands. His shoulders begin to jerk up and down.

The three circles and the oval all burst at once and disappear, just like that, gone, like they were never there in the first place and I'm wondering if they actually ever were or if I have gone totally nuts. I'm stunned by everything that's just happened and I'm replaying it over in my head to try to make sense of it but I can't form a coherent thought.

I shake off the confusion momentarily and decide I need to figure out what just happened, if it was hallucination or if it did actually happen? I should talk to the guy and ask him if what I had seen was what he was actually thinking. But how would I approach him? How do I start that conversation? As I look up he is getting on to a bus and I know that I should get on and talk to him but I hesitate. The doors of the bus close and it moves away from the kerb so any hope of answers just move on down the road.

I'm left standing and staring after it, unsure of what happened or what my questions were.

Paul Holmes

Impact

The sound of the impact had not even registered with him before he was on his back looking up at a hole running from the roof, through the upstairs of the house and the ceiling in the kitchen. He could smell burning meat and it felt for a moment like there was a weight on his chest but both faded as quickly as they had come. He lay there staring through the hole. It was encased by destruction. Pieces of debris falling away from its edges, consisting of tiles, slates and broken timbers from attic and ceiling joists. Water sprayed from a burst pipe and sparks jumped from exposed electricity cables. All of this was out of focus for him as all he could see was the light that beamed through. He could sense it's comforting warmth bathing his face. He heard a scream that felt like it was coming from close by but at the same time sounded distant and started to fade. His last thought was how beautiful the tunnel of light was, how peaceful it looked.

She was cut off mid-sentence by a series of loud crashes coming from all around her and she instinctively cowered for a moment. A car alarm drew her attention to the street and through the window she could see her car parked at the kerb, smoke rose from the front bonnet and engine that were crushed towards the ground, the windows were all gone, pieces of broken glass scattered about, reflecting light from the sun and the back end and wheels were raised away from the road from the bend in the car.

She turned away from the window and her eyes were drawn to the wood and broken plaster hanging from the ceiling and her husband who was there a moment ago was gone. She moved around the kitchen island and saw him lying on the floor smoke rising from his chest and she approached shaking her head in denial, but with each step towards him a visual confirmation of the horror that lay before her. The hole came into sight as she got closer. A perfect circle right in the middle of his chest. There was no blood, the area around the wound was blackened and charred and when the burning smell hit her nose it knocked her out of her confusion and she opened her mouth and grief wailed out.

Steam rose from the ignored cup of tea on the table. Her neighbour had let herself in and after witnessing the scene inside escorted her across the street to her own house, sat her on the couch, wrapped a blanket around her and put on the kettle. She stared in the direction of the television looking at the images being shown on the news channel but not really seeing them. A red banner scrolled bulleted facts across the bottom of the screen, 'Impact. Meteor shower rains down destroying everything in its path over a 100km radius.' She knew what she was looking at should have sparked some sort of reaction from her as the scenes of devastation were immense but she just felt numb and detached.

An image of a twenty metre crater in the middle of a road came up onto the screen with flames flowing from within; a burst gas line was leaking and was ablaze, streaming fire into the air like a flame thrower. The windows of nearby houses were all shattered by the shockwave the impact had sent out, cars had been flipped over and people were hurled through the air. Large meteors had impacted all over the devastation zone and the smaller ones like the piece that had come through her house, were parts of the larger that had broken away when they had come through the atmosphere. They had been on the edge of the devastation where the smaller impacts were surgical in comparison to the larger one.

A local news team that were reporting on the devastation were trying to get injured people to give their accounts of what had happened but most who were approached couldn't speak, clearly in shock. The camera panned to a man who was helping a woman through the debris of a nearby house. They both were covered with soot and ash, the woman held back from stumbling by the man whose head was bleeding. The reporter approached them and instantly started throwing a barrage of questions at them and shoving a microphone towards them expecting a response. The man told both to go away as he continued to help the woman along, who didn't even look at them and seemed unaware that someone had even spoken to her. The reporter ignored the request to leave them and continued his line of questioning. The man stopped them both, and slowly making sure the woman was steady on her feet, let her stand on her own then turned to the reporter without saying a word landed a punch just below the reporter's ear. The reporter's body went limp and he crumbled to the ground, unconscious. The camera followed the man who reclaimed the oblivious woman by placing her arm around his neck and they continued on their way. The camera got one last shot of the collapsed reporter before the feed returned to a shocked looking female anchor in the newsroom. A confirmed dead-counter was now a permanent fixture in the bottom right of the screen as the red banner displayed, 'Breaking news. Shopping centre destroyed by large impact, hundreds feared dead.' The screen switched to a live feed of the shopping centre. Emergency services were trying to deal with fires and secondary explosions and organised rescues had just begun with the police, army and members of the public working together to move rubble from the safer areas of the collapsed building, searching for survivors.

She vaguely heard her neighbour's voice coming from the hall in hushed and alarmed discussion with someone so she focused in on the conversation and heard her say,

'What do you mean there is no body?'

She got up from the chair and made her way to the door to see what was wrong. A paramedic was standing at the door, the strain of the day clearly visible on his face. They hadn't heard her and were unaware of her approach as she came up mid-sentence.

'……. you are aware that filing a false report is a serious offence. '

'I didn't file a false report, why would anyone lie about ….'

'What's going on?' She said, cutting them off.

'This man has just come over from your house and he says….'

'There is no body ma'am, we have searched the entire building and there is no sign of a body anywhere.'

She looked fixedly at him for a long moment and said,

'I don't understand. What do you mean there is no sign of a body? He is in the kitchen. Under the hole in the ceiling'

'Well ma'm, it isn't there now,' the paramedic responded with a snap. He caught himself and said, 'I'm sorry ma'm, it's been a very long and, difficult day.'

'I don't understand' she repeated, 'where could he have gone, who would take him?' Her voice was growing firm, anger replacing the numbness of moments ago.

'Who would take him?' she said again as she barged out past her neighbour and the paramedic and ran across the road to her house, burst through the front door and made her way to the kitchen where she was stopped in her tracks. There in the middle of the kitchen floor below the hole in the ceiling was a slightly smouldering crater where the meteorite had broken through the floor, but her husband's body was no longer there. She stared at the spot where he was, confusion and disbelief growing inside her. The other two arrived a moment later and knocked her out of her introspection.

'He was right here', she said and pointed at the hole in the floor, 'right here. Did you send another ambulance, got it mixed up and some other crew came and took him?'

'I have already checked that ma'am, no one else was sent.'

'Then where the hell is he ....' she began to yell and stopped distracted by something to her right.

'The door was closed.' She said as she looked at a lace curtain blowing with the wind.

'Did you open the patio door when you came in?'

'No ma'am, the door was open when we entered.'

She ran out the patio door to the rear garden and almost fell back with shock. Floating vertical one metre above the ground was the body of her husband. He was facing away from her, his head was tilted forward, and his arms were outstretched from his torso with his legs hanging straight and together. The blue of the surrounding sky was clearly visible through the hole in his chest. The exit wound made by the meteorite was larger than the entry at the front.

Her neighbour and the paramedic had followed her out to the patio and were equally shocked at the vision before them. Her neighbour dropped to her knees, blessed herself and still staring at the revelation began reciting a prayer. The paramedic stood there, eyes wide and mouth gaping with the colour drained from his face. For what felt like an eternity they stared and as they looked on, movement started from inside the wound. The motion roused the paramedic into patting the pockets of his coat and pants until he located his phone which he withdrew and after a series of taps on the screen held it facing the floating body. From the top and the bottom of the cavity growths began to form and after a moment of motion, vertebrae throughout the spinal column were growing towards each other and when they met in the centre of the wound fused together. The bone and sinew protruding from the exit wound began to move slowly to meet the newly formed spine, ribs joining it and setting into place while organs regrew behind it. Once the skeletal structure of the back had reformed, tissue and muscle began repairing, weaving back together and healing. The cavity disappeared as they looked on in disbelief. As the flesh joined itself from each side of the former hollow, the skin began to form in much the same fashion, slowly covering the flesh until it met itself also from each side. As the skin turned from an angry red to match the colour and tone of the rest of the upper body he slowly floated back to the earth, three heads and a phone following the movement. His feet nestled gently into the grass garden as his arms lowered to his side and his chin rose from his newly reformed chest, it swelled as he took a deep audible breath. After a brief pause his head moved slowly as he took a look at his surroundings. He turned and faced the paramedic who was still holding up the phone and studied him for a time in silence, his eyes moving the length of his body from bottom to top. He next turned to the neighbour who was still on her knees still holding her hands together from the prayer she had stopped reciting, and looked her over also before finally turning his focus to his wife. He stared into her eyes and with a look of recognition he smiled and said 'Hello dear." She held his gaze for a second and looked down at the burnt hole in his shirt; at the chest that had been vacant moments before and back to his smiling face, before her eyes rolled up into her head and she fell to the ground.

Paul Holmes

Acknowledgements

To my family, friends and the writers' group, for your support and encouragement, thank you. Paul.

KAREN SLAMMON

Biography

Karen Slammon is from Clara and is a member of Wordsmiths since 2017. She is an S.N.A by day and passionate about writing the rest of the time.

A self-confessed sci-fi and fantasy nerd, she confesses to be lucky enough to be able to write in the same genre as she reads.

She lives in a crazy household with her husband Shane Fleming and their two children Alex and Millie and two furry cat babies, Zelda and Raven.

Some of her greatest pleasures in life are, a good book, a great laugh, family and friends (normally partaking in a raucous meal) or a good girly road trip (anywhere! even IKEA).

She hopes that writing will eventually build a pathway to her dream of owning a house by the sea that will also house her ever expanding TBR (and RR) pile.

NOTHING VISIBLE

A sense of wrongness stole through the air, spoiling this perfect evening, nothing visible, just tangible.

Birds still chirped in a nearby willow tree, dandelion clocks floated lazily by, briskly chased by a zipping dragonfly. The sun hung low, nestled in copper and indigo clouds. A huge toad thrummed deeply from the mirror stillness of the pond, velvet bulrushes gently creaked back and forth.

I sat on the weathered garden bench; a faded patchwork throw lay across my legs, ostensibly to chase away the creeping chill. A fly lit gently on my arm and began to crawl up; I shooed him away with a wave of my antique lace fan. Drops of condensation slid down the glass of my long-forgotten drink.

I cast a glance at the lush meadow. Nothing stirs, but I can feel it. Out there something watches, and I am alone here, all I can do is wait and I am done running. Insects sail across the ponds murky surface, vying for supremacy, unaware that they are soon to be dinner for the pike, meandering beneath. Tiny glimmering stars pop forth, piercing the gathering mantle of twilight. I hear a truck rumble, echoing across the valley. A crow wheels on a vent of warm air, cawing nosily, breaking the stillness. I exhale, only now realising that I'd been holding my breath. Relief trickles through me. The threat has passed for now, but it will return, it always does. My rigid grip releases the throw, now crumpled and twisted.

I smooth it back across my legs, adding to the reassuring weight of the gun in my lap.

Karen Slammon

AFFIRMATIONS

The mind is a powerful tool,

For all people, clever or fool.

What can we be, what we believe,

Can be anything the heart conceives.

With the power of positivity,

telling yourself to just believe,

can open, oh so many doors,

Futures, possibilities and so much more.

Saying aloud an affirmation,

being aware of its connotation.

Seems like such a little thing,

but what bountiful blessings it brings.

Karen Slammon

MEMORIES LIVE ON

Hello! can you hear me?

I know you've passed on.

But hope still remains,

That you haven't quite gone.

Butterfly flutters into sight,

Making a day a little more bright

Gently reminding, it brings a smile.

Keeping company, stays for a while.

Deep in our soul, hope resides,

As part of our loved ones, remains inside.

Robin red flits, hopping beside,

Bringing old memories, forgotten, alive.

Darkness lifting, grey clouds brushed along,

Pinpoints of light, pulsing and strong.

Sending a message, loud and clear,

Have faith, Remember, and I'll always be here.

Karen Slammon

Solace

Waves of salt kiss the rocky shore,

Rolling shingle adds its music,

Beating a rhythm, even and slow,

Balm to a fractured soul.

Crouched on a grassy outcrop,

Velvety carpeting, soft beneath.

Salt spray, kissing the brow,

Bestowing nature's benediction.

Brushing away a salty trickle,

Leaking from a squinting eye.

Watching through wildly whipping hair,

A golden highway,

Shimmering towards arcs of sand.

Great sheets of blush and copper.

Smudged swathes of steel and ink.

Tasting salt upon soft lips,

Wistful.

Karen Slammon

I DREAMED A DREAM

I dreamed a dream,

My house was clean.

Perching nicely on the settee,

I indulged in some rubbish TV.

A loud clatter shook me awake.

Oh good Lord! What a mistake.

"Mam, we made breakfast by ourselves!"

Chaos reigned on every shelf.

On awakening properly, chanced a look,

Holy wheelie, reality struck.

Made a smoothie without a lid,

Down the wall's banana slid.

Porridge burst more and more,

Dusting oat flakes on the floor.

Milk dripped down into a puddle,

linking the floor tiles like a puzzle.

The cat stepped delicately through the milk,

leaving paw prints of liquid silk.

What to do? what a mess!

I`m off to hide in the hot press.

I`ll pretend that it`s a sauna,

hiding me from mó paisti dáná.

The witchy one, for she's the leader,

dragged her brother a little nearer.

Announced, "Well, we were trying to help",

as I winced at the massive pile of delph.

As I mentally began to put stuff in,

before me stretched a toothy grin,

"Oh, Mam, don`t worry, we`ll clean up after",

I just had to swallow a burst of laughter.

Karen Slammon

TURN KEY

Turn key, walk free,

Not so simple as that you see.

I stand before the door.

My heart battered and sore.

Go on, get out,

I’ve told myself many times before.

He always says” turn that key,

And I will never let you back to me”.

I am so afraid to leave this house,

Instead remain quiet as a mouse.

I see the kids play unaware,

From their seat, on the stair.

Hiding my misery and pain,

Knowing it will happen again.

How did we come to this?

No laughter,

No hugs,

No kiss.

Two peoples love totally broken,

From words, so carelessly spoken.

All those things that he would say,

Chipping my confidence away.

Making me feel smaller than dust on a shelf,

Locking me away inside myself.

Turn key, Turn key,

No point willing it to be.

Could I be so strong?

And try to get along,

With my life,

And little ones.

Braver now!

I have the when and how.

Decision made to just go,

Time stops and slows.

I grab the bag beneath the stairs,

Grab coats and brush hairs.

Quickly! Now, no time to wait,

The taxis stopped outside the gate.

Determined now, I turn the key,

Step out into the world that's waiting for me.

Today's the day, My very own key,

I have awoken and finally broken free.

Karen Slammon

RADIO TIMES

Time is a funny thing, gone in the blink of an eye, some say.

Isn't it strange how ripples in time, resurface, bringing long forgotten memories alive. Coincidence, I wonder. Shane was in the attic checking out some problem with our water tank, when he discovered an old transistor radio. It belonged to my parents and we brought it with us when we moved in 16 years ago.

It was a small Panasonic radio, with a handle, no headphone attachment in those days. It would be positively antique to nowadays youth. With its on /off flick switch and tuning dial to physically tune in whatever radio station you desired. A red light on the corresponding needle would illuminate when you had succeeded. A choice of s/w,m/w,l/w,f/m was also available via switch.

The aerial was broken, we had replaced it with the spiral dough hook from my Mother's top of the range tangerine Kenwood hand mixer. It worked a treat, remaining an integral part of the radio for many years, and probably remains lost in the bowels of our attic.

Immediately, I was transported back in time to the housing estate where we lived in the 80`s and the early part of the 90`s. The soundtrack of my teenage years wound from that radio beneath my duvet in the darkness of my bedroom. It was the era of pirate radio stations and that little radio picked up them all, Sunshine 101, Atlantic 252, Radio Nova (not the original) and our very own Radio West.

Most of these stations coincided with the advent of the original *Now that's what I call music* and we're up to 90 odd at the mo. (how old am I?). I miss those times when the only worry was pressing the play and record button simultaneously to cut out the d.js voice at the beginning of a favourite song. In my mind, the old neighbours strolled past, some dead and gone. With a familiar pang, I remembered the children we played with, now grown, some with grown families of their own and others passed on. Halcyon days of endless summer and great fun, first loves, no loves, foolish escapades and the lasting friendships that shaped us into the people we are today.

My parents called unexpectedly. Shane declared "You'll never guess what I found in the attic, ye're old radio", immediately taking my Mother back to her time as the monastery housekeeper. When she left one of the monks gave her the radio as a thank you for her years of service.

"Is it working, coz the one we have is shite" Mam announced." I spend more time in the morning tuning in Shannonside, it`s driving me mad".

Climbing back up the ladder, Shane re-emerged from the attic with our family heirloom. On opening the back, we discovered the batteries still there, dead obviously.

"I don't suppose you have the lead" said Dad.

"Knowing that lad, he never threw it away" Mam added knowingly.

"You need a figure of eight lead for that" said Dad" I think I have one at home,"

"Try that", Shane said, triumphantly extricating an old lead from our basket of old mobile chargers and acres of phone extension cords.

Our eyes grew wide with childlike wonder as the lead was a perfect fit and with a flick of the switch, lo and behold, static. The radio was still working.

We could identify some stations despite the old device valiantly struggling to maintain signal.

"I don't suppose you have me dough hook," Mam laughed as simultaneously Shane arrived with my whisk attachment and placed it in the missing aerial port. The signal intensified tenfold. Perfect. We were delighted, unified in memory of those long-forgotten days, frozen in time in a transistor radio.

“What’s the story with this one Gran??”

Rita Weir stood at the kitchen sink, washing and drying cups with her brisk efficiency, casting a glance backwards at her granddaughter with a mischievous grin. “Ah, that’s a good one, be with you in a minute,” she answered fondly.

The ancient leather suit case lay open, spilling its contents on to the centre of the smooth polished table. Old photos, black and white, sepia and garish 1970s throwbacks, snapshots of life, jumbled in together. The musty scent of ink and paper combined with the ever-present scent of baking. Cassie Weir sat at the table, legs curled beneath her, chin resting on her fist as she idly scanned the images taken by her grandfather. Tom Weir was the town photographer, capturing the local history as it happened. She loved to run her long thin fingers across the smooth squares, selecting images to view. Photographs had always fascinated her, especially the story behind the shot. Amber evening light splayed across the stone floor, miniscule dust motes lazily swirled and spun within.

Cassie studied the image that had caught her eye. A family photo, it struck her because of its obvious formality, the people within were stiffly seated in the parlour, dressed in their Sunday best. The two small girls in party dresses and oversize bows, both boys in flat caps mirroring the style of the patriarch. There was no joy in this photo, as both parents and children wore very serious expressions, bordering on stern. *No wondering what’s behind the smiles in this one*, she remarked to herself.

Cassie was momentarily distracted by her Pops, outside industriously pruning his roses, before taking up his Canon 500 Powershot to snap away at the colourful blooms. “That man, he just loves taking pictures,” Rita smilingly observed, jolting Cassie back in the moment.

“C’mon Gran, who are these stuffy people?” she asked. Just as another family portrait caught her eye, curiously similar in dress but a very different emotion emanating from it. Taking her own seat beside Cassie, Rita smiled, placing both photos side by side, “Here, have a look at these and see if you notice anything,” she asked

"Apart from the obvious happiness on their faces, Did Granda supply the clothes?" Cassie replied.

"Ah now there`s a funny one, "chuckled Rita indicating the first photo "Now this here's Guard Coy, coy by name most definitely not coy by nature, big, brash, totally unpleasant. He`d threaten all the youngsters with the *Black Hole* in the barracks, if they did any wrong, sure weren't they too naive to realise that he was lying!"

"I take it you weren't a fan then Gran, that's not like you." Cassie laughed; she could always tell when Gran was really warming up to the story telling.

Obvious disgust crept into Rita`s voice, "A bigger thick you couldn't meet, unless of course it was his wife Cora, now there was wan with notions, if she was chocolate she`d ate herself. She loved the status of living in the Barracks and having a housekeeper, on Silver Street, she was."

"What were the kids like? they look kinda sad," Cassie noted

"Sure, how could they be any other way!" Rita exclaimed, "Poor children weren't allowed to mix with any of our children, except in school. Other than that, they were kept apart from the rest and spent all their time in the Barracks garden. Anyway, next door stood Rose Cottage, Sonny and Julia McEvoy lived there, with their four children, two boys and two girls, the same ages as the Coy children. Sonny worked in the flour mill as a labourer and Julia did a bit of sewing to keep the family ticking over".

"Were they nice?"

Rita smiled "Sonny was a rogue with a glint in his eye and Julia was mischievous and full of fun, but they were good people, hardworking. Well Ms Cora, she just couldn't bear having *these lower-class neighbours*, she was always complaining to any who would listen about how the kids were so dirty and too noisy."

"Ah stop, seriously! go on," Cassie urged, curiosity getting the better of her.

"Well, the final straw came when Julia's nanny goat escaped and ate Cora's entire flower bed and her fine linen table cloth off the clothes line. Cora Coy in a most unladylike fury, leapt the gate of Rose Cottage and a screaming match ensued between herself and Julia, after which an eternal frosty silence descended". Gran guffawed loudly as she paused for effect.

"What a tale Gran!" Cassie leaned back and squinted her eyes at Rita who sat there ,a smug smile on her thin lips. "There's more isn't there," Cassie prompted, indulging her Gran`s taste for drama.

With a slight nod, Rita began, "Any way, Sonny used to say to Granda in the pub, Tom, someday you'll take our phota but only in our finery. One Thursday evening, Guard Coy sent for Tom to come to the Barracks and booked him to take his family portrait that Sunday after mass. Saturday morning, Mrs Roche had the Coys Sunday best washed and out drying. Guard Coy and his family took off for Fair day in Moate. A knock came to the door early, when I answered it there was little Annie and Jimmy McEvoy. Says he, *Sir, I maen Mrs, me da and ma want to know if you'll come and take our phota, like now.* Tom and I ambled on over and when we got there, there they were in the garden beneath a blossoming apple tree. The kids seated on upturned fruit boxes, happily chattering away with Julia and Sonny fussing behind. *Rita would you tie up that goat or she`ll be in the middle of us*, Julia said, Rita reminisced fondly.

"I remember admiring the girl's lemon cotton dresses and the handsome boys in their smart tweed waistcoats and matching hats, I leaned against the house as Granda took the photo. Julia whooshed the kids inside straight away calling, *Rita I`ll make tea in a second, I need to get these off them or they'll wreck them.* Julia slid the heavy black kettle over the top of the stove to heat as she rushed in to the bedroom to change herself and the kids in jig time. God, Julia those are so smart, where did you buy them? I called. Julia came back out of the room, with a wicker basket in her arms; and headed back out into the garden, indicating with a toss of her head for me to follow her. *Here, hold this* she said, winking cheekily as she thrust the basket into my hands. Well, let me tell you, the shock I got as Julia efficiently hopped the wall into the Barracks garden, and promptly began hanging the clothes back on the line. A giggle of mirth escaped her lips, her infectious mischief dissolved my shock and our laughter spread through the quiet garden."

Mouth agape, Cassie stared at Rita . “She what……. like stole the clothes!!!!!!”

“Not at all, she merely borrowed them, just making the most of the day that was in it….” grinned Rita, raising her eyebrows.

Doubt crossed Cassie`s face.

Rita observed the sceptical look on her granddaughter’s face. “I know what you’re thinking, but I haven’t lost any of my yesterdays yet, a Grá. It wasn’t done maliciously, merely out of necessity. You had to live in those times,” she explained getting up from the table, crossing to the window and called Tom for tea.

“So, go on, tell me, did you tell anybody?”

Crossing the kitchen to flick on the electric kettle, Rita replied, shrugging, “Never, when the Coys returned that evening from Moate, Mrs Roche had taken in the laundry and pressed it. The next day Guard Coy and his family had their family portrait taken, dressed in their (*already worn*) best. If Cora Coy had known she would have had an apoplectic fit”.

Cassie cringed, her hand over her mouth, “Did Cora ever find out?”

“No as I said, Julia and Sonny weren’t that kind of people, but I’m sure they had many a smile to themselves, every time, they looked at that photo, as did me and Granda”, Rita replied fondly.

Cassie heard her granddad stomping mud off his boots on the mat outside the back door.

“Sure, he has the secrets of the town inside that old head, here he is for tea, let’s have a slice of coffee cake as well “Rita leaned forward, softly patting Cassie on the hand,

“Pick another Cass, Granda will tell you the next one.”

Karen Slammon

Hands

Hands made to hold,

Hands made to guide.

Hands made to wipe,

Tears and sadness aside.

Hands made to sew,

Shoes neatly stitched inside.

Hands made to knit,

Pieces with love and pride.

Hands made to comfort,

Hands made to soothe.

Hands made to hug,

Through sickness or bad moods.

Hands always busy,

Hands made to clean.

Hands seldom resting,

Working often unseen.

Hands made to support,

Our burdens to share.

Hands helping others,

Providing comfort and care.

Hands made to discipline,

Often to enforce rules.

Hands made a home,

Safe and secure.

Hands on our shoulders,

Love everlasting.

Hands always present,

Gently guiding times passing.

Hands joined in final prayer,

Resting in silent repose.

Hands a gentle reminder,

That love forever flows.

Hands suddenly appear,

So frail and so small.

Belying the strength and purpose,

Of one who cared for us all.

Karen Slammon

The Fisherman

There is a pond, so vast and great.

A good bit further from Peter`s gate.

Above, it`s surface is mirror still,

Reflecting only the distant hills,

Beneath, bars of silver glide past,

Swishing and swirling, slow and fast.

Deep within the land of heaven,

was Our Lord and Tom Fleming.

In a boat, the two men sat,

The conversation,

Matter of fact.

"Tom, my old friend,

of you I was ever fond,

Where would you like to travel?

From this my golden pond?"

"My Lord, there`s nothing in life,

like the river rushing past.

To forget your troubles and your strife,

As you watch a line you cast.

I have ever served you,

Throughout my life and will.

If you could only grant me,

A fishing spot upon the hill".

Smiling the Lord said, "Alright my boy",

And with a wave of His great hand,

Took Tom to where the mighty Moy,

Weaves through Mayo`s land.

On the bank, Tom strolled along,

Enjoying the peaceful sight.

His hands clasped behind his back.

Looking for a spot to settle,

Sure, here's just right.

Tying on his handmade fly,

The river swirling fast.

He starts to remember time gone by,

With barely a ripple as he cast.

One thing that gave me such great joy,

Was chatting and telling tales,

Giant, medium and wee.

Many a time I told the lads the tale of Sam Magee.

What else gave me greater pleasure,

I can never say.

Reading oh so many books,

or bowing my head to pray.

Another thing, that I surely know,

I love to watch my garden grow,

Tending my plants with a gentle hand,

Coaxing them forth from God`s green land.

But, pondering on life's mysteries,

Bring such memories, don't you see.

From my little home in Silver Hill to

Working in BOPA and Ranks flour mill.

How lucky was I to be blessed from heaven?

A fine family of eleven.

Four daughters, seven sons,

And of course, above all my dearest love Helen.

Abruptly a salmon on the end of the line,

Hooked with a glimmering swish,

Granting the fisherman's greatest desire,

He`d caught the king of fish.

Now, I know that you can see him there,

The evening sun upon his face.

The people he met throughout his life,

Will never forget his grace.

I don't doubt that he`s up there,

sitting by a fireplace,

regaling old friends with stories and tales,

and a couple of poems in case.

For us he will always be father,

We are so proud to be part of him.

His legacy of wise words,

Forever inscribed within.

And though our hearts are broken,

Our sorrow raw and sore.

We are so privileged to have had our Da,

as all we needed and more.

Now it's time to say goodbye,

But this we know from high.

He will forever watch us still.

Our wise fisherman on the hill.

Karen Slammon

Acknowledgements:

There are so many people to thank, I don`t know where to begin. To all who have helped me on my way to this proudest of moments, If I haven`t mentioned you by name, know that you have my profoundest thanks.

To my family, I am eternally grateful for your never-ending support and love, my parents, Pat and Joe Slammon for their constant encouragement. My sister, Isla, often my harshest critic but always my greatest supporter.

My two children, Alex and Millie, who bring me such joy and such hair pulling moments in equal amounts. I love you.

My husband Shane, You are my everything, thank you for sorting the house and kids, thus allowing me the time to indulge myself and write what I love

To Pauline McNamee, a creative writing tutor and friend. You have given helped me more than you know.

To Geraldine O Neill, thanks for all your help and advice, it has proved invaluable.

To my wonderful Wordsmiths writing group, without your creativity, support and laughter, I wouldn`t be part of this book. You have helped me in so many ways, both personally and on my writing journey.

To my friends and extended family, thanks for all your support and good wishes. Remember I`m cataloguing all those conversations for future reference.

LORRAINE DORMER

Biography

Born in Douglas, Isle of Man, towards the end of World War 2 but moved to live with my Grandparents in Clara, County Offaly when I was 4 years old.

At 17 I moved to London starting my first job as Secretary to The Administrator of The Centre for Aged Jews. One very defining moment as I witnessed the pain and distress of many Holocaust survivors. On mature reflection I believe this experience shaped my thinking and led me to a later career in politics.

I joined the Labour Party in 1964, inspired by the first Harold Wilson Government. In 1972 I was elected to serve as Labour Councillor on Wiltshire County Council, the last bastion of Conservatism. In 1976 both my late husband and I were elected as Councillors to the then Thamesdown District Council.

Following the untimely death of my husband in 1978 combining Council duties with a full time career as Communications Manager in Royal Mail proved challenging due, in part, to a lack of affordable child care. Despite the challenges, both roles provided me with the opportunity to study Politics, Marketing and Public Relations. My career progressed through the dizzy heights of political public relations and political research.

I returned to Ireland in 1991 looking forward to a contented early retirement but the best laid plans etc don't always work out. The untimely passing of my husband, Geoff, in 1995 had a devastating affect both physically and psychologically which propelled me into a world of solitude, escaping into the world of literature, a pursuit I had long forsaken combining it with my passion for genealogy.

Joining a Creative Writing Class facilitated by Pauline McNamee, gave me the motivation and inspiration to shake off the dusty doubts about my writing. At the conclusion of the class Wordsmiths Tullamore was formed. A more committed or dedicated bunch I've yet to meet and I owe each and every one of them a huge debt.

LETTER TO MY GREAT-GRANDMOTHER

MARY SUSAN DAY (Nee Holliday

Dearest Grandmother

My family history is almost complete but I have a few gaps I would like to fill in and you are the only family member who can help.

The biggest piece of the puzzle has confounded many in both our family and in my circle of genealogy contacts. According to census returns in the U.S.A. completed by both your son, William and your daughter Jane, you were born in Connecticut, which I believe to be true as your son, Patrick, my grandfather who raised me, spoke of your family in U.S.A. That you were born in the U.S.A. is, in no way in question but where your life from the age of eleven years takes an amazing turn of events is a source of great bewilderment.

On 31st January 1857 you arrived in New South Wales, Australia accompanied by your father, John, your Mother, Mary and your three siblings, having left England, Durham to be precise, on the steamship 'Emma'.

What prompted your father to return to England? Was it because he and your Mother, Jane, were both from mining communities? Perhaps the opportunities for miners in Australia were more lucrative and offered a better future.

I would love to know about your life in Australia and what the conditions were like during the 1850's and 1860's. The only assumption I can make is that the Holliday family prospered to some degree to enable you to travel back to England towards the latter part of 1866, a voyage which was to change the course of your young life yet again. My heart skips a beat when I envisage your meeting with my Great-Grandfather, Thomas Day, on board ship, falling in love, marrying on board that ship and eventually coming to Ferbane, County Offaly, where all of your children were born and raised.

Although you had a short life it certainly didn't lack adventure. I visit your final resting place in Ferbane and I am dictating this letter to you in the hope that our souls can communicate on a spiritual level and you will be able to help me complete my search.

Please give my love to all our ancestors. I hope they are aware of the immense pride we feel for their courage, their determination and, above all else, for being responsible for our existence.

With all my love.

Lorraine

MIND'S EYE VISION

I see you in my mind's eye as you walk purposely yet wonderingly through the freezing fog of a London morning in late January, as your mind and memory try to recall the last resting place of your only brother in this overly populated community of souls. Clutching the flowers in your chilled hands you must surely be asking your God, your Creator, or your brother why this pilgrimage could not have been delayed, deferred, or postponed indefinitely.

Your great strength of character, married to your enormous generosity of spirit and your courage, echoing through the whispering willows, waving their tendrils in harmony with the ageless oaks, the stately yews, the shimmering shine of the silver birches as they join in the joyous sibilant sounds of the blackbird as he tries to out-sing the robin, delivering a balm to soothe your psyche and, perhaps, disperse some of the suppressed sadness and feelings of loss.

Row after row. Nameplate after nameplate. Each one a reminder that the owner of each identity badge had occupied and shared a space in this place we call Earth for whatever their allotted time span had been and a salutary reminder of the temporary nature of the human condition. Age, class, creed or nationality of no importance here. All equal. No up-sizing. No down-sizing. No upwardly mobile. No societal values to worry about.

As you left that place of tranquillity and whispered your farewell with the promise of a return visit, my mind's eye is seeing and feeling the weight of unshed tears, their outpouring confined to the innermost core of your being. My soul is feeling the connection between your brother and you as you fly across the Irish Sea and I hear him say, as he often said before....."You're a good girl, Sis. Not just good but the best of the best."

Written in tribute to my wonderful daughter, Sarah Mahon, whose unselfish and caring disposition never wavers. Her heartbreak at the untimely tragic loss of her only brother, Paul, always taking a back seat as she comforts the rest of us.

Lorraine Dormer

STARS

Just lately I hear some precious words

Come sounding through the ordinary drone

That is my life.

They sing the sweeter song

And prove once more that nothing is but change

As a golden blade of sunlight

Through the thatch

Or an Alpine petal in a Burren cleft

Here now, when every night sky has been tossed with its infinity of flashing stars

There will be one, however I may look

That shines and blinds and calls a lover's eye

And says 'Up here! Up Here! I'm here for you

To guide you through the storms of all your days!

And show you to my heart with all your ways"!

Thank you, my dearly departed friend and muse, Ivor Redmond, whose wisdom, guidance and amazing wit I miss.

Lorraine Dormer

I AM

I am music

Life is music to me overflowing with deep emotion. I am life in one great powerful symphony.

All of us whether as an individual or part of a group is an orchestra. Each of us playing a different part of a song.

I am like Victor Hugo "an expression which cannot be put into words and which cannot remain silent".

I am, through music, speaking a highly evocative language playing a major role in influencing society and individuals.

I am, through music communicating in a language penetrating beyond the mind, going directly to the emotions.

I am defining a moment with the power to express and convey my thoughts, my hopes, and my fears.

I am, through music, a universal language

Lorraine Dormer

A LOVED POSSESSION

My computer, my constant companion
I watch the letters forming words
Carrying themselves into sentences
Days drift dreamily by
And magically a tale is told
As the words carry themselves to sentences
To paragraphs
To stories.

For me computing has been a progression
From typing
To processing
To impression.

At my computer I am Monet
I paint my world
My life unfurled
Or, I book a holiday
Accompanied by an on-line date
No iPad
No tablet
No phone
Gives me the same space to create
This world of endless possibility.

Lorraine Dormer

OBJECTS AND BELONGINGS

When first I saw this growling bundle of fur I knew my beautiful toddler son would want it. A rather expensive toy this furry fellow was far beyond my means at the time. The Angel of Toys heard my silent plaintiff prayer and answered me in the form of my being offered additional freelance contracts.

Delighted to have the means to buy this much wanted teddy bear and knowing the joy he would bring put a spring into my step and I hurried to the shop. Growler came home to a delighted toddler who lavished sloppy kisses and hugs on him over the years. Growler was quite noisy when he growled, not liking being put on his tummy, which caused much amusement.

More than 50 years later Growler has travelled far and lived in many houses. He sits benignly clutching one of his arms which, through the course of much hugging, has become detached. He can still growl if I accidently turn him over but as he approaches middle age he is surely allowed that little quirk.

He is more precious than gold or diamonds and will, hopefully, remain so through the next generation. Sadly his owner is no longer with us but the treasured memories of their time together will endure. If I were to be parted from Growler the remaining pieces of my heart would shatter beyond repair.

Lorraine Dormer

A TASTE OF CHILDHOOD

I have carried my childhood with me right through my almost seventy-five years. My mind refuses to let me 'grow up'. In my mind and subconscious I am definitely down there with the pre-pubescent playful boys and girls. A symptom of a misspent childhood seeking to erase the loneliness or an attempt to put down a fresh life canvas with all of its possibilities and permutations.

In recalling my childhood a thousand thoughts come thundering through my mind and memory as I attempt to gather together the sweet, the bitter, and the sour tastes of a very unconventional childhood.

I come from a land beyond the sea, a tiny island in the middle of the Irish Sea, to be precise. Island people are different to mainland people.

Despite being so young when I left the Isle of Man to live on another island – Ireland – my memories are sharp and, in some cases, incisive. All of my senses are heightened as I recall my early childhood. As I think of that time in my life I feel I am being transported in a time capsule. I recall how the sea-salty smell invaded my nostrils. The screech of the seagulls and the waves as they lashed against time worn, weary rocks, assaulted my ears. These emotions are so tangible I believe I can hear my Mother calling me to collect my seaside toys. The promise of ice cream tempered my reluctance to leave the vast playground.

We left the beach and criss-crossed the busy Douglas Promenade. I grasped my Mother's hand so tightly as if to prevent me from any known or unknown separation. I am amused by the noisily neighing horses as they clip clopped along carrying the happy holiday makers in the sleek shiny trundling trams to seek out even more pleasurable pursuits.

The tinkling of the ice cream seller's van gave me that warm, fuzzy feeling of anticipation which can only be captured in childhood innocence. At four years old how can you be expected to choose from such an array of colours or flavours? In time honoured tradition, my Mother, like all Mothers, knew just what to choose for me. The taste of the sweet strawberry sauce occupied all of my thoughts. It dripped, not so daintily, onto my clothes. In an effort to avert even more mess I concentrated too much on finishing my ice cream. It dropped unceremoniously onto the feet of a passing stranger. To weep and to wail was my only known response, given my limited library of words. It stopped as quickly as it began with the promise of a trip to the cinema and an assurance that I will get another ice cream once we are seated in the cinema.

Climbing the steep stone steps to the cinema my Mother held firmly to my hand lest I should take a tumble. Safely inside the cinema my hand was released. My Mother extracted coins from her purse which she gave to me to hold. She put her purse safely into her handbag.

"Give the money to the lady, please" she said as she lifted me up.

In exchange for the money I am handed two pink tickets and a picture book. My Mother took hold of the picture book. Back at ground level I could see so many people as they waited in turn for their tickets.

My Mother loved the cinema. I cannot but wonder if the frequent trips to the cinema were a reminder to my Mother of a time prior to the outset of war when my father was a cinematographer before he and she joined the Royal Air Force. The cinema had become a palace of escapism for my Mother. I guess she took her love of movies to the brink by naming me after a movie star.

We took our seats. Despite the darkness I could see the 'ice cream lady' as she slowly took each step towards us stopping to serve the many outstretched hands. My Mother tried to assure me that I would soon get the promised ice cream. Childish impatience was not calmed until the little tub of ice cream with its wooden spoon was handed to me. The sweet vanilla taste and the cool creamy texture caressed my tonsils which banished the fear of the dark and the noise I have carried the taste of childhood throughout the years.

Lorraine Dormer

LONDON – A PLACE I KNOW SO WELL

Languishing lazily in the sullen not-quite-sunrise, eyes closed, ears adjusting to the sudden sibilant sounds of the birds as they perform their musical entrance into the joy of another day entices me to join with them.

The peace and security of my surroundings punctuated by the desire to explore, once again, the ever-changing, yet ever constant, memories of living in my favourite place. A place I know so well.

Despite the passing of the decades, London, with its culture, architecture, social vibrancy and a kaleidoscopic modernity yet with a seemingly endless air of medieval mystery sitting seamlessly like its inhabitants and following the flow of Old Father Thames from East to West, North to South through its "Twenty Bridges from Tower to Kew"[Rudyard Kipling 1865-1936] can still proudly proclaim "When a man is tired of London, he is tired of life...." [Samuel Johnson 1709-1784]

Pacing the packed platform in an attempt to secure the best position to enable access to the small international bubble of busyness with the rumble of wheels on tracks echoing eerily through the tunnels the surge by anxious commuters towards the edge of the platform is electrifying. Huddled masses massaging coffee cartons the elixir of the morning. Whoosh! Shudder! Stop! "The train now standing on Platform Push! Push!" "Mind the gap."

Seat seeking to no avail strap swinging adds a certain unwanted movement and invasion of personal space occasionally affords the opportunity of interaction with another swaying sufferer.

Parks or Palaces? Delay in decision. So many choices, so little time. To shop or not to shop? Museums or Galleries? A river ride? A swim in the Serpentine? A concert in the Albert Hall? A day time dalliance in Covent Garden? A canal trip from Little Venice? A bird's eye view from the London Eye? Cranial cramp from observing the glistening glass of The Shard? Portobello market? A sporting venue? A ballet? An opera?

London, incredible, inspiring, indulgent. A genteel demure lady in Belgravia. A gutsy work weary Whitechapel gal.

Lorraine Dormer

I COULD NOT TELL

I could not tell that morning the kind of emotion you were feeling. I sensed you felt as I did. This parting would be painful. We were both anxious not to prolong the embrace and my pleas for you to take care.

As you travelled onwards and upwards to the departure lounge I glanced at your shape. I tried to avert my tear filled eyes lest you should witness my distress at your leaving.

I could not tell as you walked through the automatic doors that it would be the last time I would see you. I could not tell what pain you were in. You couldn't or wouldn't tell me of the seriousness of your condition.

I could not tell of the horror which would visit your sister and I in the few short weeks after your leaving.

I could not tell why the seriousness of your condition was not prioritised and acted upon.

The Coroner could not tell what had led to your tragic and untimely death or its cause.

I could not tell my pain. It was. It is, and will forever be, indescribable.

Lorraine Dormer

THANK YOU FOR A GOOD DAY

There was 'Peace' in the sinking sun

That sank as day was nearly done....

I saw it near the silent mere

As, after one short day of cheer

And warmth that touched on us today,

Earth sighed to sleep – Youth ceased to play....

I passed some youths just sitting still

And talking calmly – not of ill

Intent or most malicious deed;

Attuned to 'Life'; appraising need

As they perceived the moment then –

As they shall do in 'Age' again....

The breeze was hushed yet vibrancy

I sensed in all 'Life's' infancy....

'Joy' pulsed in every small, tight bud,

In stem and leaf – within the mud –

Beneath the water's surface glass! –

From whence some bubbles rose to pass

Into the silent symphony

To praise fresh 'Hope' for you and me.

Pink clouds....

A hint of rain to fall

Before the Sun – that fiery ball –

Shall rise to warm us yet again....

But such sweet drops will not constrain

This 'Life-force' bursting for release

Yet succour in new 'Love' and 'Peace'!

I shall cry in gratitude –

Not whisper lonely platitude....

And so I do – and look above –

In thankfulness of chance to 'Love'

Thank you, Geoff for so many good days.

Lorraine Dormer

A Life defining moment

January 3rd 1949. My birthday and I'm starting school.

My Granny is trying to come to terms with having the full time care of a very young traumatised child of whom she has had no previous knowledge. She is at a complete loss as to how to console me but busies herself preparing breakfast whilst at the same time endeavouring to impart to me the great time I will have when I get to school. I can feel the terror of leaving the warmth of my new home and Grandparents but know with certainty this will happen.

Grandfather senses my fear and tries to remove some of the fear by singing a song and telling me funny stories about 'Swank' our dog and 'Muskin' our pony.

"Come on, now, be a good girl and put your coat and hat on...we don't want you to be late on your first day, do we?"

Everything is so new and strange to me. As we walk to the school I see the vastness of whiteness all around and wonder at the excitement of the other children on their way to school. They are sliding on the icy road fearlessly but I cannot join in as I clutch my Granny's hand so tightly for fear she will disappear.

We arrive in the school yard. No playgrounds then, just a galvanised shelter and outdoor toilets.

"You have to go inside now to your class."

"Don't be upsetting yourself, the time will soon pass and it will soon be time to come home again. When school finishes you can walk home with the other children but don't be sliding on that ice or you'll break your leg."

So many children all around and I am completely bewildered by the way they speak. I am the sole object of their curiosity as they cannot understand the way I speak.

Nuns.

I have never before seen a nun and the black outline standing at the top of the classroom reminds me of the pictures I have seen in "Little Red Riding Hood" and my vivid imagination kicks in leading me to believe it's the *'big bad wolf'*.

Cowering down an apparition approaches me and takes me none too gently to the top of the classroom and, as the swishing of the leather belt and the jangling of the very big rosary beads conjure up dreadful images, I am mentally trying to re-trace my steps. Steps which will lead me back to the safety of my Mother's arms.

"We have a new girl here with us today. We must all give thanks to God that this little girl has been rescued from sinners. All of you in this class must teach this little girl to pray and learn all about our ways."

"Go back now to your desk."

Rooted to the spot I look around at a sea of faces in front of me and I am immobilised with terror because I don't know where my desk is.

"Go back to your desk."

"Now girls, you can all see how we have the sin of disobedience being committed."

Feeling as if my feet are stuck to the floor and before I can try to 'make' them move I am propelled with the aid of the blackboard pointer to my desk.

"Hands up all of you who can write numbers."

Almost every small hand is raised but mine is not one of them. I know all my numbers up to twenty. Mummy showed me how to count by using my fingers, toes, ears, and eyes.

"Come up here to the blackboard."

Shrinking into invisibility I am unaware that this request is for me.

Once again I am roughly removed from my desk and placed in front of the blackboard.

Watching all the other children taking out little slates and chalk I wonder if I should be writing on this huge blackboard.

Swish......swish.....swish! The leather strap is swaying from side to side and then hits the wall close to where I am rooted. The crashing sound makes me jump.

I know Sister is telling me to do something but, as I cannot understand what she is saying, I start crying - something I had promised myself I would not do.

Sister is very cross with me. Children always know when a bigger person is angry with them. Angry eyes are frightening eyes.

Some other children start giggling which distracts Sister's attention away from me as she leaves my side to go and terrorise the little victims of laughter.

Rap....rap...rap! The classroom door opens and a man in black enters. Terror temporarily suspended.

"Good morning children."

"Good morning, Father."

At least I can understand what this man in black is saying but wonder if all the adults in this strange place wear black.

"Now, children, you all know Jesus loves little children and you all love Jesus, too. There are so many children who do not know about Jesus so we must pray that the good Sisters, Brothers and Fathers will bring all those little souls to Jesus."

"Have you all brought your penny for '*The Black Babies*'?"

A chorus of "yes, Father" echoes around the classroom and Sister takes the little box and collects the pennies.

I know Granny gave me a penny when she left me in the school yard and I put it in my coat pocket but I am too terrified to speak up so I try to stand still and remain invisible.

"God Bless you all, now, children and don't forget to say your prayers and obey your Mammies and Daddies and all the good Sisters who teach you. I will see you all again next Monday."

"Goodbye, Father."

Sister places the chalk in my hand with such force that the chalk snaps in two and I am pushed so close to the blackboard that I can feel my nose against the cold surface.

Tap...tap...tap!

The pointer is roaming across the blackboard on words I cannot understand. It looks like all the other children are writing on their slates but I am still nose-pressed to the blackboard.

My chalky fingers are directed to the words and I draw squares and make them into little boxes. Mummy always told me "I was such a clever girl because my squares and boxes were so neat and straight-lined."

Slap...slap...slap!

The ruler makes contact with my legs.

Push...push...push!

Marched unceremoniously back to my desk and, despite the stinging pain in my legs, I am relieved there will be some distance between Sister and I.

Ding-dong...ding-dong...ding-dong!

Rustle...shuffle...rustle!

Slates and chalks hurriedly put away and children arise from their desks and push and shove each other towards the classroom door but I am, yet again, rooted as if the chair is part of my body.

"Come on its time to go outside to play. We can make slides on the ice in the playground. We can walk home together, too. My house is near your Granny's."

Trust comes so easily to little children.

My fear subsides and I take the offered hand of friendship as we walk out into the school yard.

There are so many children all happily engaging with each other and playing their games. The noise is deafening to me but I still manage to hear my Granny calling me as she stands by the school gate waving her arms. I try to run but slip and slide across the yard.

"Come here to me allanah. Ye poor children are frozen. We'll go over to the shed and you can have your suppa tae and I've brought you an egg on toast."

Other children mill around Granny and she tries to share out the tae. Loaves and fishes!

I am very aware of the envious looks from some other children as I eagerly eat my food.

Searching in my coat pocket for my hanky to wipe my hands I find my penny.

"Oh Granny! I didn't put my penny in the box for *'the Black Babies'* and Sister will be very cross with me."

"Don't be fretting about that now, mavourneen. Can't you give it to her when you go back in?"

"Please, Granny, don't let me go back in to Sister. My legs are sore and Sister is very cross."

"What ails yer legs, child?"

"Sister slapped them with the ruler."

"Did she, now? Well, we will soon see about that. Your Grandfather will deal with Sister and that's a promise."

Ding-dong...ding-dong...ding-dong!

All the children are trying to run across the icy school yard to get into line for their respective classes. I am in no hurry to join this stampede and am still clinging to Granny's legs in the vain hope I will win a reprieve.

"Come on, child, you have to go back into school or I will have the Priests and Nuns coming to the house and I don't want any of that trouble at my door. School will be over soon and you won't feel till you are on your way home to your Grandfather and me."

I am the last child to take my place in the classroom and am very aware of the many faces looking at me but keep mine firmly fixed on Sister as she paces up and down.

Tap...tap...tap...!

No words are spoken as each desk in the classroom echoes to the rhythm of the blackboard pointer and as Sister returns to take up her place at the head of the class the children shuffle as they, each in turn, stand up.

Sister starts singing and soon, as each child joins in, the classroom becomes a less fearful place for me. I love singing and although I don't know the words they are singing, I soon pick up the melody.

"Loudly the notes of the trumpet are sounding

Proudly the war cries 'arise' on the Gaels.........." [O'Donnell Abu (Michael Patrick McCann 1824-1883) written about Rory O'Donnell, 1st Earl of Tyrconnel]

Clap...clap...clap!

Stomp...stomp...stomp!

Hands clapping, feet tapping, voices in unison follow Sister's lead into another song.

"The Harp that once thro' Tara's Hall......" [Thomas Moore, 1779-1852]

As the notes of the song fade away Sister raises her hand and I follow the actions of the other children as they sit down and place their heads on their desks.

Sssh...sssh...sssh!

There is total silence as Sister speaks.

"Angel of God

My guardian dear......"

"Hail Mary

Full of Grace......"

I am happy to join in with the other children as I know these words. Mummy always said them when she tucked me up in bed at night. I've heard Granny and Grandfather saying them too but they kneel in front of the big fire with their rosary beads.

Ding-dong...ding-dong...ding-dong!

Despite being told by Sister to walk quietly I am unsure of where I am meant to be going but my new found companion takes me by the hand.

"Come on, it's time to get our coats and go home."

"I don't know the way to my house."

"I told you already I live near your Granny's house and we are walking home together so stop crying or the bigger girls will tease us all the way home."

As we slip and slide up the hill and down the other side, chat about the games we can play together and exchange stories about the toys we have, my fears subside. I am happy to be out of school. In my innocence I don't realise I have to go again tomorrow and many, many, more tomorrows.

The walk home seemed to go on forever but eventually I see Grandfather waving from the gate and I leave my new 'best friend' and try to run and slide towards waiting arms.

"Thank you for bringing this poor little child home from school" . Ye are frozen and it looks like snow is on the way so get yourself off home now darlin' and tell yer Mam and Dad I said 'you are a great girl' and sure I'll tell them myself when I see them."

Granny is at the door beckoning us in and I feel the warmth of her greeting easing away my anxieties.

"Come on astoir and wash yer hands. There's a lovely hot dinner waiting for you. When you're finished yer dinner you can go with Grandfather and bring Muskin in from the field so that he won't be frozen in the snow."

"Granny, can I bring Swank with us to get Muskin?"

"Of course, you can, a gra and when I've made sure the hens are safely locked away from Mr Fox we'll settle down for the night and keep warm. If you're a good girl you can stay up to listen to Dinjo and 'Take the Floor'." No television way back then. The wireless was the ultimate in home entertainment.

Grandfather and I walk through the frozen fields till we hear Swank barking and running around in circles. He has seen Muskin who comes galloping towards us.

"Come on now, pet. I'll lift you up onto Muskin's back so that your little legs won't get too tired from all the walking."

"Grandfather I'm scared of Muskin and I might fall off."

"Don't be fretting yerself. Isn't Muskin the quietest little pony there ever was? I'll walk along with him and there won't be a bother on you."

Once I feel safe on Muskin's back I look up at the sky. It seems to me that I can almost touch the stars as one by one they start to twinkle as if they are winking at me.

Yap...yap...yap!

"Why is Swank making that noise, Grandfather?"

"That fella's like a child, he wants to get up there with you."

"That is so silly. Dogs don't ride horses or ponies."

"Well this little dog can do anything and you can teach him some new tricks."

"Whoa, Muskin! Let me put this dog up there with the child."

"Move back there a bit, pet, and make room for Swank and don't be frightened. Muskin and Swank are great friends and they won't let anything bad happen to you."

We gently trot back towards the house as dusk begins to wrap us together as one.

"Run along in now, pet and tell your Granny 'all the jobs are done for today'."

"Granny, Muskin carried me and Swank all the way home and I never fell off."

"You can do that again tomorrow when you get home from school."

"But, Granny, school is finished."

"Ah, God love you, pet. You've plenty of years at the schooling before its finished."

I cannot say I ever fell in love with the concept of school. Well, definitely not the time I spent with the Sisters of *No* Mercy. The days, weeks, months and years were tolerated and no more than that.

The relentless regime of both prayer and punishment suffocated my spirit and can only be seen, with hindsight, as complete strangulation of the senses.

Despite this, or, perhaps in spite of the endeavours of the Sisters some of us managed to adopt coping mechanisms. A few of the braver little souls, in the full knowledge of the consequences, sought at every opportunity to challenge the system of thought repression.

School, like life and its living, is never one-dimensional.

The ten years I spent in Primary School taught me much more than the core subjects of *Reading, Writing and Arithmetic*. I tend to think they shaped and formed my character. The coping strategies I learnt during those years have served me well.

The 'nature versus nurture' theory had not been widely expanded upon back then. Had it been, I believe the theorists may have concluded that 'nature' was the outright winner.

The ability of children to create and furnish many rooms in their minds has and will, continue to astound me.

"In my Father's house there are many mansions....."

"Suffer little children to come unto me...."

My carefully created *'mind mansion'* still remains intact. I have designated it as an *Area of Special Conservation*. It has been adapted, extended and re-decorated many times. The exterior life storms have threatened its foundations from time to time but the emotional insurance policy I took out as a young child has allowed me to repair any damage within a relatively short time span.

"I am a captain.....You're my First Mate....We signed on together..." [The Voyage, Johnny Duhan, Songwriter, Author, Musician and an amazing human being].

Continuing Education

The harshness of the school regime had its many compensatory times.

Walking to and from school provided a fertile oasis for the imagination. Games were played, friendships formed, secrets exchanged and peer rivalry had its daily outing.

Children will always have an acute perception of social or religious divide. They have a greater insight than adults and an innate sense of looking beyond social construction. It was certainly so in my young world.

The daily doctrine delivered by our teachers that all but people of the Catholic faith were *pagans* and needed to be saved held little sway outside of the school environment.

In the little town of Clara, where I spent my formative years, I cannot recall any religious divide. As children we knew and accepted that children of other faiths than our own attended separate schools and attended a different church for worship.

Nature or nurture theory?

Goodbody's and Ranks Flour Mills were the chief employers in Clara at that time. This may have influenced attitudes and afforded the opportunity to look beyond the narrow perspective of religious difference.

At that time, too, there were many ex-soldiers who had served in the British Army in World Wars 1 and 11. They, through necessity, had no option but to connect and relate with people of different cultures and religions. Whilst they may have left their home town with a narrow parochial view of society, they certainly returned from war with an overall world perspective.

I have vivid recollections of my late Grandfather holding court with neighbours and friends as he described his army time in India, Palestine, Turkey, France, South Africa and Serbia.

The knowledge gained from these hearth and home discussions instilled in me a hunger for information about peoples of our world. No book or movie could depict more clearly the capacity for human beings to bond, irrespective of class, creed or colour than when presented with a common purpose.

The abundance of spiritual wealth far outweighed the material poverty which prevailed in virtually every home during those years. There was an abundance of resourcefulness to be sown and reaped at every life stage. “Necessity is the Mother of invention” was certainly put to the test at every level.

Necessity created and sustained a large skills pool within the community. It was a professor of many life faculties with a full compliment of students.

As Primary School students we progressed through each class, most of us in innocence, longing for the day when, Primary School Certificate examination completed, we could leave the hallowed halls of the Convent of Mercy.

For most of the students formal education ended at the age of fourteen.

An extract from my as yet, unpublished, book ‘Happy Days and Hollidays’.

Lorraine Dormer

ACKNOWLEDGEMENTS

My thanks, in no small part, go to Pauline McNamee, Creative Writing Facilitator. Pauline infused all of us with her beautifully calm approach to teaching. Wow! Pauline you're some woman for one woman. In the year when we celebrate the achievements of women and the enormous struggle of so many who went before you epitomise the essence of womanly worthiness.

To my daughter, Sarah Mahon, who has been my rock and anchor, Thank you for always encouraging and supporting my many foibles and, at times, crazy notions.

Had my beloved son, Paul, still been with us for this writing adventure he would be cheering for Wordsmiths Tullamore. His love of literature might have propelled him to join us.

Geoff and Eddy, my two soul mates, each with their individually distinctive styles and use of language taught me so much about the use of English both plain and classical. Thank you both. Yes, I did listen. I know the comma rule better than anyone on the planet....."***If in doubt, leave it out.***"

Thank you to all my friends. You know who you are.

So many people have inspired, motivated and energised me during the compilation of our stories, poems and memoirs. I would like to give a special mention of gratitude to Siobhan Gorman who has proved to be such an asset. A more eager, committed and willing student would be impossible to find.

A special word of thanks to Paul Holmes who unselfishly ploughed through the proof reading with me. You are such a valued member of Wordsmiths Tullamore.

Finally our group could not have embarked on this writing journey without the help of all the staff in Tullamore Library. Thanks to each and every one of them.

Here's to **WORDSMITHS TULLAMORE!** What a great bunch you all are. The creative talents you continually demonstrate are beyond belief.

MARY LYNAM DUNNE

About the Author.

Born in Tullamore, Co. Offaly, Ireland, where she still resides,

M.L.Dunne is a retired Drama Teacher, Stage Director, and Photographer, who has now turned her hand to writing.

Many of her short stories, plays, poems and essays have been published over the years.

She is also the author of four books to date:

- The Blue Stone
- The 10.15 Train
- The Secret Temple
- Rock Pools.

The mind is a vast uncharted territory and most of us never penetrate into its rich hinterland. Become pilgrims of the mind. You are not journeying into the unknown: you are simply seeking your inner self. Take that wonderful voyage. Write down what you see, how you feel. Let your words speak out without fear of discovery. You are unique in so many ways. Let us enjoy the passages of your mind. Free the beauty that is within you.

PROCRASTINATION.

He hid himself well within the shadows of precaution.

And called himself 'friend.'

He spoke loudest when she held her dreams aloft for him to see

And was silent as she saw them fly away.

He stole the essence of her soul

The ka of her being

The psyche of her mind

And left her emotions open to the storms of time.

Her dreams shattered under his influence

And she bathed in the twisted reflections of

What might have been?

What could have been?

What would have been?

What should have been?

But where was Procrastination in those last tragic moments?

When Precaution cried out one last time?

And he robbed the world of her beautiful thoughts.

Mary Lynam Dunne

THE ISLAND OF INIS SCÁTH

The girl sat on the beach. Her legs curled beneath her, her hair blowing in a light sea breeze. Attuned to the sounds around her, she listened to the waves, the gulls, and the wind, the crash of water against rocks and the forever jingle of the sea shells as they struggled to break free of the crevices in the rock pool into which they had fallen. The boy beside her was restless and began playing with the soft sand underfoot. He built small mounds, and then began adding a series of moats and pathways to his creation and whatever other imaginary things he could think of. This occupied his mind for all of five minutes, then dragging his foot across the sand he levelled the area only to start rebuilding all over again. She paid little heed to him, as her eyes scanned the mist that lay between the sea and sky. She had detected a noise on the horizon, a noise that she was unable to identify, a noise strange to her island home. The boy heard it too and rose to his feet with fear. A dot appeared far out on the ocean.

'Go back to the village.' She ordered. The boy did so without argument. Grabbing his discarded jacket he fled across the sand and up onto the small road leading from the beach. Clambering over stone walls he took the shorter route until he reached the top of the cliff. There without looking back, he disappeared from view over the brow of the cliff face. The girl stretched her long legs in readiness for flight, but was held back with a powerful curiosity. The dot grew larger. She was not afraid for in her heart she knew that this visit was inevitable. Had she not predicted it some time ago, as did the holy man, Sireco and now it was coming to pass. The dot took on the shape of a small cabin cruiser. Its engines screamed inside the girl's head, for it was a sound that she had seldom heard. There were no engines on the island, the loudest noise here was that of the wind in the trees during a gale, or the crash of the sea on the cliff face during a storm. This was not a welcome sound.

On the far left of the beach as one faced out to sea there was a small jetty built against the side of the cliff, which jutted out into the waves. It was used very little now, not since the mainland ferryboat stopped coming to the island many years ago. The girl was too young to remember the ferryboat, but not too young to know and understand what was happening now. She watched in silence as the little cruiser drew alongside the jetty. A young man emerged. He tied the boat firmly to the bollards before looking about. Though she had never met him before, she knew instantly who he was and how much she hated him. Their eyes locked for a second and in that instant he felt her hostility and a chill stirred his insides. She watched him come onto the beach and walk towards her. To her dismay he walked through the rock pool and not around it. Her anger grew for that was hallowed ground to the islanders, a sacred place, and he had not given it the proper respect. His shoes sank into the soft sand as he continued on his way towards the road behind her. Though she could no longer see him, he knew that she was fully aware of every step he took. Her acute senses followed him up to the edge of the beach and onto the road. There he stopped suddenly and turned back towards her, had she just spoken to him, or was the voice he heard inside his head? Looking down he saw that she was still staring out to sea and hadn't moved; yet the question was repeated.

'Why did you come back to the island?' it asked and without thinking he heard himself reply aloud to it, 'To bury my father.'

The girl lifted her head and looked directly at him accusingly. He turned away and continued to walk up toward the village. It wasn't long before he found the house where his family used to live. To his disappointment he discovered that it had not changed in any way over the last fifteen years. The stone walls and thatched roof still smelt of burning wood, the chimney breast black from use. In the sparse interior the furniture, though meagre, had been beautifully carved by loving hands. Regardless of its lack of modern day comforts it was neat, clean and comfortable inside. Nothing had changed; it was as if time had stood still on the island. The frugal lifestyle of the islanders had survived over a hundred years and though he disagreed with their way, he had to admire their spirit of protectiveness. The community had grown together in such a fashion as to eliminate the need for any contact with the mainland; they had formed a colony of their own. Steeped in their own code of behaviour and spiritualism they had merged into a true Celtic society. A definite hierarchy existed in which everyone knew their own place. He knew that he was no longer a part of their world. He had forsaken that when he crept aboard the ferryboat fifteen years ago and ran away to the mainland, though only sixteen at the time, no older perhaps than the girl on the beach. He had turned his back on the old ways. Here among them again he couldn't help but feel some remorse for their wretched ways but he was glad of the choice he had made on that day. He had worked hard and success had given him the chance to enjoy the remaining years of his life with ease.

The sound of approaching footsteps brought him out into the hazy sunshine again. From where he stood at the top the hill he could see the spiralling cortege as it wound its way from the shoreline, through the gap between the fields and across the base of the hill. As they walked, they carried his father's dead body high upon their shoulders. The spectacle un-nerved him as he watched them draw near. Their reverence was reflected in their chanting. He had not realised that so many lived on the island and it took perhaps ten minutes for the procession to pass. Many of the faces were familiar to him but none greeted him or acknowledged his presence. Towards the end of the line he saw the old man, his hand resting on the shoulder of the young boy that lead him safely along the path.

'Serico' the visitor uttered quietly, 'don't you recognise me?'

The chanting stopped instantly. The walkers stood in frozen silence as if waiting for a signal to continue. The old man turned in the direction of the speaker. Sensing the man's presence, he closed his weary blind eyes for a moment, and then said quietly to the boy beside him.

'It is the voice of a dead man.'

With that, the chanting was resumed and the group moved on.

From the shelter of a stone wall the girl watched the funeral go by. As it passed the old cottage, the tone of the chant changed and became more thrilling. The stranger seemed to wince with this new sound. No one looked at him or spoke to him. She knew this had to be so; he was not one of them, but none the less he boldly stepped into line with the cortege and followed it up to the small circle of stones, inside of which the funeral pyre awaited.

The mantra grew in intensity as the body of the dead man was carried to its final resting place. In the eerie half light of the failing evening the torches set the base alight and the cremation began. With each rising flame came the most frightening sound the young man had ever heard. It grew with such intensity that it un-nerved him. The entire spectacle made his flesh creep. Had it been the funeral of anyone other than his father he would not have returned to the island. The behaviour of the islanders had become more bizarre in the years he had been away from them. Their thinking was not of his world, the modern world and he had moved on but here on the island the inhabitants, it seemed, had fallen further back into the ancient habits. Their spiritualism feasted on the way of the Druids and the adoration of the Gods of Mother Earth. It frightened him to witness this, though he strove not to show his abhorrence of their culture.

As the embers burned into the night, fanned by a cool sea breeze, he sat aside and watched the many displays of reverence and grief the people made in honour of his father's passing. It was surely rewarding to see the respect they bore him. He knew that had he remained with them, he too would have been rewarded in this way, but he had made his choice many years before and knew that he would never be accepted back into their lives again. The vigil continued through the night and into the early morning. By five the following morning the man's energy was ebbing and he left the stone circle to return to the family house. There, on a firm wood based bed, he lay down and drifted into a restless sleep.

At nine the following morning he suddenly sat upright. The sense of presence in the house was overbearing. Grabbing his jacket from the back of the old wooden chair, he hastily put it on to ward off the coldness that had invaded his bones. Looking around he saw nothing of a personal nature in the house, no memento that he could bring back with him in remembrance of his father and Mother. It was as if they had never lived there, never existed. Had the place been picked clean by the other islanders? If so they had done it well. On the tall wooden dresser the crockery lay in neat display. The cups hung from their individual hooks, each set as it were in geometrical correctness. Everywhere was crude but clinical. Even the bed had been neatly dressed; the beautifully carved headboard with its broadness and height gave little hint of the firm hardness of its lay. And it was this that gave the young man some thought. Lifting away the firm horsehair filled mattress, he studied the sturdy base. There was a depth of three inches in it that suggested to him the presence of a cavity of sorts. Gingerly he ran his fingers along the sides until he found what was a small gap between the top boards and the side. Sure enough there it was the telltale sign of friction, where the board had been removed and replace many times. With a new excitement in his heart the young man smiled to himself. His father had after all left him some little token of his past life. Cautiously he slid the board away to reveal the broad opening in the top and there they were, in neat bundles side by side, his father's last gift to him. The young man's legs buckled as he slid onto his knees in shock for before him lay every letter that he had written to the old man over the last fifteen years. Each one still intact, unopened, unread, unwanted. Tears swelled in his eyes as he silently cursed the island and its people. With anger in his heart he rushed outside into the cool morning air. The sea before him was calm though misty. The gently rattle of keys in his pocket assured him that in a short while he would be back on the mainland among his own kind. There would be no more return journeys to the island, the past was over now and any connection he had with the old world had gone with the death of his father. The old man had left nothing behind for him, nor did the stranger need any reminders of his past life here on the island. There would be no goodbyes. He would simple leave as he had come, quietly and without fuss.

On the beach the child led the old blind man towards the rock pool. Inside it the foaming waters spiralled through and around its many large boulders. The sound of the sea was loudest there. It was as if the rocks themselves were giving voice to the waters, sending out a warning to all that dared to approach that this was hallowed ground. Serico held no fear of this and allowed the boy to lead him inside. There he touched the crusted stones and listened for the message of the ocean before taking out a small leather pouch from which he shook out the five dried bones that were his sacred oracles. As they fell to the soft wet sand, the waves swept across them briefly then pulled away.

'Tell me what you see' the old man asked of the boy, who at once explained how the bones lay. 'It is as it should be' Serico added in a voice that held no malice or regret.

The early morning sun glistened on the moving surface on the ocean. The young stranger looked out to where the sea and sky met; soon he would be out there, alone on the silent sea feeling the power of his prized boat shudder under his feet as he steered away from Inis Scáth and back to the material comforts of his chosen new homeland. The past was dead to him now; he had paid his last respects to his father and none on the island could reproach him anymore.

At first the beach looked vacant but as he drew closer to it he could see the girl, the same girl that had appeared to speak to him yesterday. She didn't look up as he passed but continued to look out to sea. At the far end of the beach the boat was still tied to the jetty, rocking gently on the morning tide. It was only when he came to the rock pool that he first noticed the old man.

'Serico,' he uttered, 'I am leaving now.'

'Why did you come back?' the girl asked once again. The stranger turned around to face her and was surprised to see that all of the islanders had gathered in the distance and were watching from the cliff tops and from the road.

'I told you' he replied sternly, 'to bury my father.'

'Your father's spirit died when you left fifteen years ago.' The holy man said.

The stranger made no response.

'You will take nothing of the island with you.' Serico advised.

'I have nothing to take' he snapped back, 'nor shall I ever return.'

And with that he continued across the beach towards the jetty.

'You will take nothing of the island with you.' The girl added sternly.

When he looked back towards her he was confused, for she was still sitting some distance away and yet her voice was strong and clear inside his head.

'I have nothing to take' he yelled, 'I want nothing from this place.'

'You are your father's son.' The old man said almost in a whisper.

'What?' gasped the younger man, 'what are you trying to say?'

A low chant began to rise from those watching, at first it was only a murmur that floated down from the cliffs on a breeze.

'You were born of this island' the holy man continued, your father was our King; you carry his blood in your veins.'

A silent gasp caught in the young man's throat. He looked into the eyes of the old man with disbelief. The chanting grew in intensity; every sound reverberated inside his head. He covered his ears with his hands in a vain effort to block out the awful hum.

'You will take nothing of the island with you.' Both the girl and the old man repeated.

It was then that a terrible fear filled the young man; he felt his heart beating against his ribs and with a sudden surge of energy he tried to run towards the boat but the chanting held him back like an invisible chain. It entered every fibre of his body, tormenting him, tearing him apart, he couldn't stop the heartbeat, and he couldn't slow it down. His breathing came in gasps now as he struggled with the pain building in his chest; it seemed as if his very blood was trying to break away from him.

The islanders watched as he sank to the ground and when he finally lay still, the chanting stopped.

A few days later, a passing trawler saw a small cruise boat adrift on the ocean, there was smoke coming out of the cabin, but before they could get to it, a sudden explosion rocked the little craft apart and it sank beneath the waves. No survivors were found.

THE END

Mary Lynam Dunne

LOST LEGACY

The pain of separation

Still fresh on my bruised heart

Catches my every breathing moment

And drives me to believe in your memories.

Your thoughts striving to help me

Keeps me struggling to maintain your legacy,

A gift that faded in the harsh reality of uncaring leaders.

Gone now the security of your presence

The wealth of your knowledge

A gift passed down that burst on impact

Before the magic of it could cast its spell

But you were richer in your youth than me.

For you had the unclouded open mind of innocence.

You enjoyed your Irishness with pride

Before it was given away to others with foreign tongues.

Cheaply sold, along with our dreams, our hopes and our futures

By those we trusted in our ignorance to believe in Gods justice.

What now is to become of the new poor?

Those of us left to lower our heads and our expectations

In the hope of seeing another day.

Mary Lynam Dunne

The Mouse

From

A little hole in the corner

He comes sniffing,

twitching, scratching

Tiny feet

pitter-pattering

Sliding, slipping on smooth polished surfaces

Brown furry coat like silk, shimmering in the shadows

Dark eyes shifting, studying, piercing the night

Little ears listening, tuned in, twittering

At first darting, now pausing

Scurrying, skulking, sneaking

Prying hiding bidding his time

Whiskers piercing the night like feathers

Brushing the wind.

Long tail, ever swishing, ever following

From shade to shade, across vast empty expanses of plush carpet.

Sensitive nose quivering, exploring the air

Smell of food, cheese, Gold

A mountain of it

A blinding

Yellow

beauty

Gotcha,

Snap,

Squash,

Gone.

Mary Lynam Dunne

THE WILLIAMS' FARM.

On the narrow country road the intensity of the rain increased with intense ferocity. It was as if the elements were enraged with each other. Lightning strikes spat out at the open fields as the thunder urged it on with deep angry roars. The road seemed to quake with fear as the soft grass verges struggled to keep back the torrents of water that were gushing across it onto the gravelled surface. The lone driver, in the old ford escort, fought to keep the car on the road as he trudged his way towards the next village. Pausing, only, to check the crumpled map beside him on the passenger seat. He was fuming with himself for having come on this weird journey in the first place, yet curious enough to want to continue. The darkness of the storm and the slow progress he was making gave concern. Should he fail to see the village soon he would be obliged to pull into the side of the road and spend the remainder of the night in the cold car. A prospect that he didn't wish as he had brought no food and was already feeling the chill of the evening. Then he saw the beacon of light just a short way off the road. Following his instinct and with renewed expectation, he sought the short avenue on his left that led to the welcoming light. Within a few moments he could see the farm. A well kept place with an open yard and sheds and a fine two-storey house. The sign on the open gate read, 'The William's Farm.' The brightness of its well-lit windows gave him a sense of relief as he gingerly drove into the yard and drew alongside the house. Pulling his jacket over his head for protection from the driving rain, he dashed the short distance to the large red door and knocked. In less than a minute the door was opened and he was face to face with a most charming little girl. She smiled at him and called out to her Mother. The two welcomed the stranger into the house. Following a brief introduction the man was invited to join the two at the table and a warm meal was set before him. He soon discovered that the lady of the house, Mrs Williams, was recently widowed and ran the farm with the help of her young sixteen year old daughter, Roisin. A labourer from the nearby village was hired to come by each day for a few hours to help with the heavier chores. Though it had not been easy for them, they had managed so far to keep the farm running. The three chatted merrily into the night until finally it was time for sleep. The man was given a room at the rear of the house on the ground floor while the two ladies retired upstairs.

The following morning the guest awoke to the sweet smell of bacon and eggs. The ladies had also prepared a lunch pack for him to take on his journey. Feeling somewhat embarrassed as he accepted the package he offered to repay their kindness but they refused to accept anything. It was when he was about to drive away that he remembered the gift he had got made especially for his own daughter and was yet to give to her. Removing the small box from his briefcase he offered it to girl, Roisin. She was thrilled to find a beautiful silver chain with a ring on it. The ring had a strange symbol carved into it that she had never seen before and asked him what it was, he explained that it was called Shou, the Chinese symbol for long life. Overjoyed with the gift, she put the chain about her neck and proudly displayed it for her Mother. The woman had at first protested but when he explained that he could have another made, she gracefully accepted.

'When your daughter is old enough,' the man explained to Mrs Williams, 'She can wear the ring on her finger.'

Having made his final farewells he drove out of the yard and back onto the road. At the gate he had to pause and pull aside to allow the farm labourer on his horse and cart pass through. The man didn't appear to notice the car at all.

Sometime later, when the car driver finally reached the village, he stopped at the tavern to make inquiries about his intended destination. The town, to which he was going, was still some way off and the barman informed him that, due to storm damage and fallen trees, the road was closed and he would have to wait for it to be cleared. He estimated that it would take perhaps two hours before any traffic could get through. A little irritated with the delay the man ordered a glass of beer from the barman and sat up at the counter. Though still early morning the place was reasonably full. Many local farmers being on their way to the market and finding the road blocked had appropriately headed for the tavern instead. The conversation throughout was mostly about last night's terrible storm. Complaints of flooding, frightened animals and the odd threat of fire were discussed and the relief that no injuries to either man or beast had occurred. As time passed and the stories drifted from one table to another, the stranger became more aware of how lucky he was to have found the Williams farm.

At some time during the morning the door was pushed open and a rough looking man walked in. His entrance brought a sudden stop to the conversation and the stranger was drawn to turn and look. The new comer appeared unaffected by this and took a seat at the furthermost end of the counter. In a gruff voice he ordered a drink and the bar man reluctantly served him. The buzz of conversation in the bar resumed but was in a more subdued manner. Finally the barman decided to chat up the car driver. He was anxious to know how the man had come to be here and where he had stayed during last night's storm. The man explained how lucky he had been to find the Williams farm.

'Lucky indeed' said the barman, 'it's possibly the only shelter around here for some distance.'

'You must be starving so?' remarked one of the farmers

'On the contrary,' the car driver remarked, 'the woman of the house fed me well.'

'I thought the Williams place was empty?' the barman added and looked suspiciously in the direction of the gruff customer. The unpleasant fellow simply shrugged his shoulders, unwilling to be drawn into any conversation. The barman invited the car driver to join him and some of the farmers at a table. They were anxious to learn more about his overnight stay at the Williams farm. Gladly the man related the full account of his visit, the generosity of the two ladies and their parting gift of food. By the time he had finished his story every eye in the place was on him except those of the unsavourily fellow at the counter.

'You wouldn't be making fun of us now, would you?' one of the farmers asked.

The man assured his listeners of the certainty of his words and even produced the package of food from the car. Mind you it did seem strange to find that the parcel was wrapped in brown paper and neatly tied with string.

'Mister, we don't know what you thought you saw nor did last night.' The barman began, 'But it sure wasn't what you think.' And they went on to explain a very frightening story indeed.

It would appear that some twenty years earlier the same Mrs Williams and her daughter Roisin had been the victims of a most heinous crime. A neighbouring farmer, who noticed that the farm animals had not been fed in the last few days, had gone over to investigate. He found the mutilated bodies of the two women in the kitchen of the farm house. The entire village was shocked by the brutality of the crime and though the farm labourer, Thomas Sheedy had been under suspicion for some time, no weapon or evidence was ever found to tie him to the deaths. For twenty years now the mystery had remained unsolved.

'You must have seen a ghost or something.' One man remarked and quickly took a deep slug from his beer. The others agreed with him, for there had been many rumours of strange things happening at the empty farmhouse. The young car driver was shocked. How could he have imagined all of what had happened? How was it that he could tell them all about the widow's late husband and the little girl's fear of the handyman? The urge to return to the farm was very strong but not as strong as the fear that was building up inside of him.

'You saw Thomas Sheedy go into the farm that day didn't you?' the barman whispered under his breath, his eyes wild with wonder and excitement.

'I don't know Thomas Sheedy.' The driver whined as he studied the anxious faces before him.

'That's Sheedy.' One of them said pointing at the wretched man sitting at the counter. The spit in the young man's throat dried as the shaggy stranger stared back at him. There was a scowl of malice etched across his unkempt face and on the little finger of his right hand he wore a ring with the Shou design on it. The car driver recognised it as the one he had had especially designed for his own daughter.

'Oh my God' the young man gasped as he ripped at the string on the food package. He carefully removed the wrapping paper and found it contained, not food but a dark stained cloth inside of which was concealed a bloody knife. On the handle, encrusted in dried blood were the clear fingerprints of the woman and child's killer. Thomas Sheedy stared down at the weapon in terror. He had lived in dread of this day for twenty years.

Mary Lynam Dunne

Smile/Anger

Somewhere in my frenzied mania

My intellect remembers the pain

I shut my mind to the living

Loving the agony that was once there

Enjoying a new style of despair.

And then my heart recalls

Nothing of the grief but all of the charm

Growing up surrounded with love, while I

Endeavoured to stall

Reminders of a past age.

Mary Lynam Dunne

The Woodcarver

It was late summer and the old man was eager to enjoy the few warm days left in the season as best he could. His home was a small shack close to the sea. He kept it neat and tidy. It was well placed on the scrubland just off the sand. On the higher land above the shoreline, a small modern bungalow nestled into the landscape. At night old Ben could see the lights from its windows and it gave him a feeling of security. But the sight he loved most was the sea. As he sat outside his small home, he could hear the waves break against the rocks and stones and it comforted him. The sea, after all, was his friend. The old man had spent the best years of his life by the sea. Yet in those years, Ben Dawson had never learned how to swim. He had never been on a boat nor did he ever want to be. It was the water itself that intrigued him. The waves moving in from the horizon, building up as they came towards the land and fading away, once broken, on the shore, thrilled him. He marvelled at their power, their persistence and the glorious sounds they made on a windy night. And it was on a night such as that when he first became aware of how beautiful the moon was. She controlled the tides of the world and turned the quiet waters into whirling sprites that sent many mighty ships to their doom. At night Ben would watch the sparking reflection of her rays on the ever-restless sea and wondered at the loveliness of her painted seascapes. She too was his friend, the Goddess of the oceans. The gentle sea breeze that brushed against his cheek was reminiscent of his late wife's calming touch. The whisper of the ocean was her voice. He missed her greatly and longed to be with her again.

In daylight hours Ben would walk along the water's edge and search the sands for pieces of driftwood that he would later carve into some exclusive shapes. Shapes that bore a meaning just for him alone.

'Why do you do that?' a voice once asked from the doorway.

'Because it's important to me.' he had answered without turning because he knew the voice was in his head. A voice he recognised from the past, her voice. A sound that was now lost to him forever, except inside his head.

‘I am creating my dream catcher.’ He added with a smile.

‘You need to have some dreams for that.’ The speaker replied softly and was silent again.

And so it was that as the days passed, it became more pressing for him to complete the task he had set out for himself. Night after night, his old hands gently shaped the pieces of driftwood. Smoothing the hard surfaces with fine sandpaper, he lightly rounded the edges into a softer, warmer touch. Fine particles of wood dust floated on the air each time he blew across the piece. The glow of the fire flickered on his hands as he worked in silence and seemed to give movement to the completed pieces on the mantelpiece. His tender eyes looked across at them as he watched them dance in the heat waves of the fire below.

‘Soon, little ones’ he whispered. ‘Soon you will be one.’

In the bungalow on the hillside, the Jones family were preparing for bed. Their ten-year-old son, James, was already fast asleep in his room. Mister Jones watched his wife turn out the house lights. Across the quiet beach they could see the faint lights from old man Dawson’s cottage.

‘I feel so sorry for him sometimes.’ Mrs. Jones said wearily.

‘Why?’ her husband asked.

‘He has no one, no visitors, no family.’

‘And no one to bother him or tell him what to do.’ Her husband added in fun.

Ben Dawson held the last unfinished piece of driftwood in his hand. Turning it over and over, he studied each little section, searching for that form, waiting for the wood itself to tell him how it wanted to be shaped. Finally, he took a small chisel into his hand and began to chip away at part of the little piece.

'No need to rush.' The voice inside his head advised him. 'The figure is already there, you just need to bring it out.'

'I know that, my love' Ben answered. 'I can see it's going to be a fine piece.

The following day the beach was quiet. The Jones family came down to walk their dog. The boy, James, ran ahead chasing after the excited barking pet. The waves rolled in, silently sweeping the loose sand before it. Small rivulets of salty water ran after the tide as it slipped back into the sea. Above the soothing sound of the surf, the wind carried a gently melody. The whisper of wind through wood produced a series of musical notes. The family paused to listen.

'That is so beautiful.' The woman exclaimed and scanned the seashore for its source.

The little dog stopped running and raised its nose. It sniffed the salted air and listened intensely to the tuneful jingle. Then slowly the animal made its way toward the old man's shack. It stopped at the small porch and lay down, its tail wagged contently as it lay silently looking through the open door at the man sitting inside.

As the family approached the shack, they saw the dream catcher hanging from a post. Swinging loosely in the breeze, it sang out, as the wind passed through it, for all to hear. The many pieces caught as it were on a spider's web, each one different in shape and size. All created to catch the air. Each one a different note and pitch perfect. It was like the woody sound of pan pipes in a fairy world. The serene smile on Ben Dawson's face expressed the inner peace of the old man, who had listened to them sing through the night as his wife called him home.

Mary Lynam Dunne

In Praise of My Father

12th January 1991.

He was not a God
He never was nor could he ever be
Yet he behaved like one and in those moments
I believed that he was.
I blame myself for this
Because in my mind I wanted him to be
Greater than any other man
I created the perfect idol
Lived my youth in the shadow of
An all knowing, all seeing Tower of Wisdom.

It was unbelievable that one brain
Could hold so much knowledge.
The mysteries of the Universe
The floodgate of his mind
The riddle of simplicity
And the pure intelligence that was
His to command.

And thus he accepted the adulation of a child
And thus he outgrew the mortal skin of man
And began to believe in my fantasia.
I had manifested the icon of perfection
And saw little beyond the mystics of my own intellect
My feet remained in the earth
Never loosing touch with my own reality
But I lost the true image of him somewhere.
In the transition from youth to maturity
A developing mind overtook the fear of awe
And in the culture shock that followed
His crown slipped and the king lost favour.

The bitter realisation brought shame
And misplaced anger directed itself
Against the God and not the creator.
He was not omniscient
He was human
And I couldn't accept that.

He is king in my eyes forever
The king died on the 7th December 1995
And the child in me still cries.

Mary Lynam Dunne

That's Magic

As I watched the old man struggle in his final hours, I was moved, not by his efforts to hold on to life but by his calmness to reach out to God. The strong religious belief that he had held so preciously throughout his years, was now giving him that serenity of mind that he had enjoyed in his long life. I was reluctant to let go of my father. He had been my constant friend and advisor for so long. In those last few precious moments, I had begun to resent God and His promises of a better afterlife. I held in my hand, a small blue stone. A crystal that my father had given to me some years earlier and which I now wore on a short silver chain about my neck. There was nothing special about it, no gold setting, no sparkle, just a smooth calming surface and a roundness that felt soothing to the touch. I saw him watch me as I fingered it absentmindedly and a smile came to his face. The smile that I had grown to love so much, for it came, not just from the tiny creases of the skin and a stretch of muscle but from his loving eyes and from deeper still within this wondrous man. I remembered how his soul sang to me as we laughed and joked our way through the many ups and downs of our time. We grew older and wiser together. Now, realising that I was about to loose him, my heart was breaking but I didn't want him to know it. The blue stone brushed against my palm and raising it up to the level of his eyes, I whispered secretly.

'I still have your blue stone, Dad.'

A new radiance came to his gentle face. He uttered, in a strained low voice, what were to be his final words.

'That's magic'

And with an expression of sheer joy, he closed his eyes and left me forever.

For many years, his last words haunted me, until finally I began to realise the value of their meaning. For in those few final seconds, he had given me the basis of the many stories and books that he knew I was capable of writing. So began my journey into the world of literature. His inspiration pushed me beyond my own imagination and into a place of infinite beauty.

'Your last gift to me, Dad, was the greatest of all. Though you never lived to see it, you live in every word I write, in every story I tell, in every dream I dream. Thank you.'

The End

Mary Lynam Dunne

ACKNOWLEDGEMENTS

I wish to thank my proof readers:

Anne Gouldsbury, (Retired Teacher)

Celine Kiernan (Irish Author)

Geoff Oakley (Retired Editor)

With special mention for my colleagues in the Wordsmith Writers Group and, in particular, Lorraine Dormer.

GEORGINA GORMAN

Biography

Born in Keighley and living in Bradford England Georgina moved back to Ireland with her family in 1976. Graduating Galway College with a City & Guilds Cheffing degree she still holds a flare for cake baking and decorating. After working in hotels around Ireland and settling back in Tullamore. Georgina met and married Barty thirty five years ago, has seven fantastic children and to date ten wondrous grandchildren. Georgina always had a yearning to write, this came to fruition when joining Pauline McNamee's creative writing class in 2017. From this creative writing class and an open poetry mic night, Wordsmiths was born.

As Martha Mc Mahon kindly wrote (*thank you Martha*) "Georgina Gorman is a writer and poet whose work is filled with social commentary. She is not afraid to take on difficult topics such as suicide. Georgina gives voice to the Tuam babies. Perhaps her greatest attribute, is her ability to say so much by saying very little, she truly is the master of the short sentence."

Unending Swansong

Suicide filled the dressing room

weighing heavy on Life's shoulders.

Life stooped before a mirror,

sometimes dull

sometimes bright

today flickering off-on-off-on.

Life secured the masquerade

disguising it's reflection.

Entering stage left, Life floated

adorning a multicoloured two faced mask.

Entering stage right, Suicide performed

a mind blowing act to no applause.

As Life's performance waned

Suicide stole the limelight,

Life's mask crashed.

The audience gasped

some cried-

others guiltily left the auditorium-

many prompted Life to live.

Life slowly unfolded

on teetering steps grew,

strong pirouettes commanded the stage

pushing Suicide aside.

As the curtains fell and rose for an encore

Life shone relieved rehearsals were over

Whilst the audience stood in ovation,

Suicide

Silent

Invisible

Auditioned

another life to act upon

Georgina Gorman

BRO

Ah ha grinned the Grim Reaper

swinging his scythe with glee

a fine strong heartbeat

to accompany me.

No thank you bellowed the heartbeat

heroic paramedics shall resuscitate twice

freeing me from your gripping vice

No flat line for you today

call again

when I am old and grey.

Georgina Gorman

Sick

Taking me hostage

Playing with my mind

Ravishing my body

You were awfully unkind

Blurring night into day

As you had your wicked way

No one could help me fight you

When

last week I had the flu.

Georgina Gorman

Tumulas

My origin shrouded in mystery
Where I come from a fact
I came from down below twice
It was not very nice.

My birthplace surrounded by breathtaking landscapes
My breath taken by tyranny and vice
A town famed for its notarized offspring
Shame my presence did bring.

My death date
The 20th anniversary of men martyred in this place
fighting to rid persecution harsh rule to free
This was lost on me.

Mortals appear leaving flowers and gifts
horrified by the visions of their minds eye
Weeping as they question
How could this happen and why?
My birth town translates from Latin
the burial ground of two shoulders or burial mound
Named by my forefathers the Vikings
To me very profound.

I was buried shoulder to shoulder
forming a human burial mound
Seven Hundred and Ninety-Five Babies
*were my **blanket** underground.*

The first time I came from down below
I was birthed from my tormented Mother's womb
The second time I came from down below
I was **dragged** from a septic tank in Tuam.

Georgina Gorman

We Bough To You

Naming 796
Catherine Corless
Paid a four euro fee.
Did we fall from your
family tree?

Daydreaming

Striking his gavel, the Judge said "Mr. Ryan your case against F&F (Future Furniture) pertaining to unfair dismissal has been denied".

"Ah Jaysus your honour that's not right" shouted Mr. Ryan.

"Silence in court" the judge once again struck his gavel.

"But, but your honour you never heard my side of the story" pleaded Mr. Ryan.

"Young man I have read and studied both the complainants and the defendant's documentation as handed to my court, signed by yourself and Mr. Knobs of F&F (Future Furniture). Based on these documents of which I am sure you have read? I find you were not unfairly dismissed for daydreaming".

"Ah good God your honour, I never read anything, I just told yer man here", indicated with the nod of his head to the gentleman standing by his side, he wrote down what I told him and made me sign it".

"Well now" the Judge glared, "was it ever explained to you that you must always read a statement before you sign it?"

"Nah your honour" answered Mr.Ryan.

Sitting back the Judge swivelled his chair from side to side, with his hands posed as in a prayer, and a hint of amusement in his voice, "Mr. Ryan I certainly would not like to earn a reputation for ruling without all of the facts, so in your defense in the case of unfair dismissal, I shall give you five minutes of the courts and my time and allow you to put forward your case".

"Ah thanks your honour." Rising from his seat Mr. Ryan began "Well now your honour it's like this you honour, the first time Mr. Knobs shouted at me for daydreaming I was only helping a customer. You see this tall gangly fellow entered the store, he asked me what was our longest bed? After thinking for a minute I remembered the six-foot slumber lumber. Showing him the bed he asked me could he try it for size.

Well now your honour I took one look at them muddy trousers and shoes, and said to myself, if Mr Knobs comes out of his office and catches them shoes lying on one of his beds, I would surely lose my job, so your honour I said to yer man, you're about a head taller than me, so if I lie down on the bed, you can imagine me with two heads, one on top of the other, then you should be able to gauge if the bed is long enough to suit you? So your honour, I sat on the edge of the bed, untied my laces, removed my shoes, and as I lay on the bed, I glanced over only to see yer man heading out the door, and here I was lying down pretending to have two heads, thinking to myself the cheek of that fellow, when I heard Mr. Knobs shouting at me to get off that bed and get to work. I tried to explain myself to Mr. Knobs your honour, but he wasn't having it, so you see your honour technically I was only doing customer service.

Now your honour, the second time, I will admit been on the lash the night before with the lads, Mr. Ryan winked over at the Judge, and you know yourself your honour some sesuins can be worse than others. Well now your honour it was one of them slow days, the store was empty, looking around at the beds wishing the day was over so I could get home to mine I thought to myself maybe I should test the comfort ratings as written on the labels. The Cloud Divan had an eight-star comfort rating but personally your honour I found it too hard. The Spring King also an eight-star rating was too noisy. Then I tried the Seven Star rated Cotton Wool feel for real single, and wow I could feel my body and aching head sink further in. I was wondering would I ever have enough money to purchase one of these beds, when all of a sudden it was like being in the middle of a nightmare, waking up to Mr. Knobs shaking and shouting at me to get the feck off the bed whereupon he there and then fired me. So can't you see you honour technically I was only doing market research?"

As the Judge sat forward he said "Mr. Ryan I shall not overturn my verdict, as I would also be fired for falling asleep and daydreaming on the job. I have reached my final verdict. Mr. Ryan I shall award you one hundred euro from the poor box fund, so you can enroll in a writer's workshop, because let me tell you young man, you sure can spin a yarn". The Judge smiled striking his gavel.

Georgina Gorman

Black Block

Well here I am Jayne Fryer Best-selling Author wondering what my many fans would say if they knew the truth, trying to find the energy to get out of bed is so exhausting, only the necessity of a screaming bladder dragged me to the bathroom. Slumped on the toilet a gleaming top of the range shower enclosure beckoned. Ignoring it, I shuffled back to bed.

What the hell is wrong with me? Out there in the world I am a seller of wondrous words with followers awaiting a sequel, living in the house of my dreams. In my world words don't flow I am cocooned in bleakness, current abode... black hole of nothingness.

Writers' block what smart arse gave it that name? Sure aren't blocks useful? Oone could build a wall or a house, I probably should build a bridge and get over it. Turning over in bed consumed by the emptiness of not thinking I surrendered to the loneliness in my soul.

Surfacing from an unrested slumber, blocks still penetrating my thoughts, maybe I should build a stairs and climb out of this blackness that buries me. That's it, caught up in a light bulb moment I WILL build a stairs block by block right up to the top of this God forsaken darkness and for every block laid I shall write a sentence.

Day One.... block one laid, it felt good.

Day Two......block two laid, I can feel a glimmer of hope. Haven't felt that in a long time.

Day Three.... block three laid, patting myself on the back this was a brilliant idea. Until block three crumbles, cascading me once again into darkness.

Day seven......surprisingly enough the Doctor thought my ramblings about a stairway to freedom was a good idea. But he did say, A good block layer will only build on a strong foundation. He prescribed some medication for me; provided leaflets for me to read and recommended I talk to family or friends.

Day nine...... foundation laid and what an interesting and informative day this turned out to be. I was shocked. Family and friends actually knew about my depression! Humbled when I realized their constant phone calls and house visits were for my benefit not theirs. When I nervously mentioned the doctor prescribed me Zanex, I learned many in my circle of relatives and friends took tablets for wellbeing, Zoloft, Prozac and Lexapro collectively affectionately known amongst them as happy tablets. Solidifying my foundation was the realization that when I was in a room full of people and felt totally alone wasn't just exclusive to me.

Day Eleven.... Block one, two and three were laid with ease. A lightness wraps itself around body and mind. I am going to wallow here for a while to allow healing.

Day sixteen ... block eight laid with confidence. The fog has lifted, the veil of darkness gone. I can feel the breeze, see the flowers. Everything seems fresh and new.

Day seventeen... maybe someday I will unwillingly go back to block one, but my foundation is solid. For the now I am sitting in front of the writer's desk, my mind filtering words through pen in hand as I begin to write my sequel.

Georgina Gorman

The fly

The fly on the wall hearing stories

TALL

yarns woven through time

tales of love, fear, untruth

Omitting or adding words at will

changes history

The fly on the wall

knows mystery.

Georgina Gorman

Prayer

Telling myself it's only for fun

to entertain

But there's a lot to lose

a lot to gain

Keep calm

don't let nerves reign

Sideline believers chant my name

I can't let them down

bring them shame

The green flag rises

starting the game

It will be over soon

Pleeeeeese God:

Don't let my egg fall off the spoon.

Georgina Gorman

Reality

Arrogant Bureaucratic Collaborates Denying Enough Funds.

Goading Homeless Indigents.

Jackasses Knowingly Leaving Marooned Nomads Out.

Politically Quashing Reality.

Seeing Through Urgent Vagrancy.

Wasted Xenagogues You Zealots.

Georgina Gorman

Neglect

Apparent Benign Cervical Data Effects Females

Guilty Hiding Illness

Jesters Knowingly Leaving Mother's Needlessly Outraged

Please Question Re-testing,

Still Sent To U.S.A

Vacillating Women Xerox Your Zings.

Georgina Gorman

Am I Crowned

I have a branch representing youth with many curves from learning.

Another spotted with gall where blossom of myrtle and honeysuckle play.

Upright a branch stems relics blowing in the wind searching for faith up high, bark-less in places where sap weeps as often did .I

Jewels clutter and sway on another sparkling with friends gathered over the years rippled with love, laughter, tears.

Posterior bad apples in boxes where they belong

My trunk truly weathered rings counting many.

Beneath kindred sovereignty roots long, short, weak, strong ancestors my genealogy

I am crowned

Or " am I…"?

A branch diverged the evening I began a creative writing class

growing fast

bending with words of encouragement, deep feelings, laughs

For this my tree doth

Bough to you.

My tribute to Pauline Mc Namee, writing class friends and Wordsmiths

Georgina Gorman

Graveyard

What I didn't tell you in life

Remorsefully

Travels

Soundless

Underground.

Georgina Gorman

ACKNOWLEDGEMENT

I would firstly like to thank you for taking the time to read our book.

My contribution to Whisperings would not be possible if not for my wonderful family {which are too many to mention}, hour upon hour of listening to my writing and rewriting. I love you all.

Also my wondrous Wordsmiths family whose encouragement, kind words and belief in me is never ending.

Thank you to my long time friend Sue. We have travelled many an interesting life journey together and, by pure coincidence, this is our most adventurous.

If I were to acknowledge everyone individually I would need this book to myself! But I have to express appreciation for my learned friend Lorraine whose hard work and kindness to my daughter Siobhan, myself and all the Wordsmiths knows no bounds.

Georgina Gorman

ROSEANNA TYRELL

Helen's Unseen, Unheard Beauty

Beauty Vibrations

Snowdrift

Homework

The Bravery of Snowdrops

The Longest Day

The Blaskets

The Skelligs

Realm of the High Road

The Gentlefolk of Birds

Empty Space

Old Ghosts

Ferns On The High Bank

Honeysuckle

Pericarpus

Light From A Barge

My Father's Hands

Ploughing

Roses in Ballinagar

Biography

My name is Roseanna Tyrrell, from Tullamore, Co. Offaly. I love to collect my thoughts and memories and keep a record of the many beauties in life and in nature. They usually form into poetry, but sometimes as a run of thoughts that have rhyming words within. At times I wake up with a poem that seems to come out of the blue. I have collected these thoughts and poems and the following is a selection of some of my favourites.

HELEN'S UNSEEN, UNHEARD BEAUTY

The dance of cooling water on my hand,

To sooth when fevered from a long stay,

My day in the warm sun,

That burns upon my face,

I pace to find a bonnet or some shade;

That glade feeling again,

As if standing where cool young sturdy tree's leaves

Whisper a pattern on my arm,

Tickling their earth story,

Of what we call green,

It's smell clean, and pure,

Demure amid the scents of man.

The soft footprints of the lightweight butterfly,

"Why, she thinks I am a petal".

They say, in soft finger movements

That her beauty is like an angel on the wing,

Her tiny feet still, unsure, she's not heavy;

Already I felt as she passed, her light body brush,

No rush and on she goes.

I'm told she lands to forage amid the lovage

And geranium pots;

She stops and sups beside me.

The beauty of a circle of soft angles

Their forms, like tiny hands in prayer with the

Softness of my best velvet dress,

Small in my hand, and smelling

Of a soft summer day,

When the unseen flowers

Colour my mind with their soft sweet

Stain of perfume;

In my room, the gentle warm breeze,

Frees my world of dark,

With a language unknown to those free to see;

Rich and warm and sensual,

It caresses my skin again,

The feel of summer rose in my hand,

Kind, and in my mind, beautiful.

Roseanna Tyrell

BEAUTY VIBRATIONS

Finger patterning and spatterings of rain or sleet

Or snows that make you feel alive;

The vibrations of life,

Of wind on my face or in the trees;

Its pull and creek like chord within bark, dark,

Unseen and mysterious beneath my hands,

Rough and damp and old,

Sometimes smooth and cold;

Its smell sublime, richer, darker,

Slower and older than other patter in my fingertips;

I feel its life movements stronger than my own.

Nearby the power of the river,

That shivering tremor in the rock beneath my feet

And fleet with torrent teeming,

A shock of cold that splashes and dashes past,

That vibrates its heavy power in my silent bower,

God's speak;

Differing from the heavy beat of train or drum,

That's far heavier still than the rhythm of my heart,

That speeds and slows in my feelings of the day.

In the night, the feelings, lighter,

Save for the heart of the clock

Throbbing when I reach my hand for its cool metal life nearby.

I'm feeling young in the soft warmth of eiderdown,

Old in the cold of morning, feet upon the floor in Winter.

Roseanna Tyrell

SNOWDRIFT

Gaudi style walls, undulate along country lanes, convex, concave,

Sculpted by the wind, they weave along,

Still, serene in beauty,

With the whiteness of a pure soul

Causing a sinking, muffled, footfall.

I plod along and feel enclosed

In the great Mother's arms,

Dressed in all her Winter charms.

The blackbirds and the crows survey

The white carpet scene,

Leaving criss-cross patterns,

In their foray to find food and fields and farmlands,

Usurped in the white pristine.

The blackbird's sharp fear alarm

Tears a seam of sound through the silence.

Blizzard winds send loose powered snow

From trees, and through the white fog freeze.

The pale dying winter sun is smothered

In this white duvet display.

Written while completing a project on Antoni Gaudi during the winter snowstorm.

Roseanna Tyrell

HOMEWORK

Silently, he was there,

Amid the homework tantrums,

We tried to avoid by stealing to the hall.

It never worked,

Called to bring pens and books and all,

Like a prisoner for execution,

You sat to the red topped table,

Unable to escape the enclosing elbow to the jaw that hemmed you in;

The sharp voice, a pin in the ear,

So near she shut him out from being saviour,

And we'd waver in our young knowledge

Of English and Math;

No gentle chat, just the clammy hotness of fear,

Her voice and breath on your ear;

A knuckle to the temple,

If you came across as simple.

If the sum entailed water

Leaving from bucket at a rate,

She became irate

At your stupidity

In calculation,

The culmination,

"For Jazus sake, will you leave it so"!

The invisible echo, from behind her body barrier, And the worrier let out a breath.

When she walked away in rage

At the correction,

A rapid collection and escape!

“Let them be fools that live

In a labouring man's cottage" was her retort;

But he was our resort, if you needed

A pound for books or school expenses.

This wasn't my dream of what life should be,

But as he sat there quietly,

I often wondered what went on

Inside his head.

What he thought of that scene,

Of what was said?

I never asked, as he dozed,

No hug goodnight, to make it right

Before the books were closed.

Roseanna Tyrell

The Bravery of Snowdrops.

The bravery of snowdrops,

White flags of memory - of the sower;

They push through the frost- hardened patch,

Where he planted;

By the water pump, so many years ago,

He knelt as if in prayer,

To sow the tiny bulbs that now light the memory of his chore.

Soft white petals, brave the frost

As a new year grows.

They recall him to me, once again as before,

Busy sowing, or cutting grass or plaining timber

By the open, old house door,

Where he could view his handiwork.

They still return by that empty, open door,

And I recall those days when I was small,

Collecting curls of wood,

Sweet smelling ash or pine;

A treasured memory of mine.

Roseanna Tyrell

The Longest Day

The longest day,

Not long enough when there's sun.

When life was simply,

About games and play and fun.

Oh, I remember the longest days,

When my only responsibilities

Were to carry turf or water or guard hens,

When I confessed lesser sins, in threes;

Sorted in my head before entering,

The dark room of the soul,

To the priest patrol;

Where sanctified grace removed all trace

Of these made up tales.

I wonder if that large supply of grace

Can balance the scales

Of life lived since

I was a child?

I wince at the deficit due

And my sins I rue.

Roseanna Tyrell

THE BLASKETS

A reminiscence of giant sea mammals in slumber,

I blunder upon the scene;

The Blaskets - black silhouettes,

Against the yellow ochre sun,

Their ever changing beauty stilled,

Yet full, in the fading light.

Tomorrow, - they promise –

Another beauty day,

Sun or storm their beauty never waning.

Be there thunder clouds,

With strike of light upon their seam of rock,

Amid the grey green ocean,

A punch of beauty shock,

To take your breath away;

Safe distance from the boiling foam

And green grass cliff,

These moments 'stop the clock'.

Should the sun glow down upon those hills,

Humpbacked, in the wide expanse of blue,

Long-forgotten dwellings on Great Blasket you can view;

A glimpse of ancient, simple times,

Of fish - and flowery potato drills,

When music, meant a lapping wave, their Celtic airs or gull shrills.

Upon a hill, Peig's old ghost

With eyes upon the ferry still;

Lips moving in silent prayer,

Looks down on this family of beauties.

As varied flocks of seabirds,

Follow ancient duties.

Roseanna Tyrell

The Skelligs

Sheer rock walls,

Stand tall, where a myriad, dive and shrill

And bicker over rock space for a homely nest.

Come April, added to black crest, the puffin.

Little Skellig, all inhabitants, of the feathered kind,

Gauging space and wind,

They soar to meet the congregations

In the sky of blue;

Storm petrels, fulmar, gannet and all creed

Share food and cry and hue;

And when, not far away a new denomination,

In past years, built strange beehive huts

And steps of man's formation,

The seabirds watched, that build and dedication;

Michael the Archangel, given veneration.

Yet the birds still nest and plan regeneration,

The quietly monks long gone.

Stone crosses mark their time here,

In a line formation.

The steps no longer tread

By those of robes and sandaled feet;

And visitors come on visits short and fleet.

The church empty of the sound of chant and praying meditation;

Nights are silent, but for water sounds, nobody there in contemplation

And weather ravages, keeps council in this bay.

Bird families living still amid the fray.

Roseanna Tyrell

REALM OF THE HIGH LOAD

Inherited respect emanated, like a soft fog on the canal,

Into the bachelor silence

In the realm of the high load of spiky bales;

The silence reverent;

At twelve, I was the watcher,

Always the watcher,

But oblivious to the other's eyes upon me,

Lulled by the rocking, high above,

Where God's arena was in full view,

Flush with its colours, red and green and blue.

That sunlit silence, a windy echo

Of their warm farmhouse kitchen,

Where the spinster, bitter in pain, lived her day.

My heart cried for her

But you dare not show

A soft heart in the cobbled room,

Only the cricket could voice an opinion

And he did,

Hesitantly, as if questioning the quietness of every day;

A hissing kettle and the clock, his only competition.

But she got swept away

When Joe showed us his thumb,

Bent back beyond belief,

Attention brief, my mind soon shifting in that childish way;

It would stray to the imaginings of my brother,

Or a left leaning towards cool green leaves and shade

On a hot summer day.

[***Inspired by the many long summer days helping the neighbours bringing home the turf.***]

Roseanna Tyrell

THE GENTLEFOLK OF BIRDS

In a huddle, reminiscent of Dickensian aunts,

In soft dove grey, heads together,

The odd ruffle of feather, the resettle,

To get a better listen to the latest tale.

I oft' times wonder on what topic they bill and coo, You tooo, you, too too.

Genteel, country cousins

To the ruffians of Trafalgar or St. Marks Sq.,

Still gentle of voice

But a scrabble of wing and feather

In a rush of hunger, when old outwit the younger.

Back home the 'country cousins'

Grace a branch or wire,

With all the decorum of a country squire,

Low toned, moving with dignity

In their quiet country way,

Always in the background in the making of hay,

Or harvesting of grain;

Their necks strain, amid cool leaved branches,

Until, the field is quiet of humankind,

Then you'll find the portly pigeons swagger in the stubble amid the cut corn rubble.

Roseanna Tyrell

EMPTY SPACE

Always there, at every meal,

I noted your portion, that was never given,

Her hatred driven,

The empty space at table that should have been yours.

It made me smile, that each set of delph

Had five; then I had a sense of you alive

With your cup and plate and potion.

I loved the notion that you had your freedom, from control, your parole,

From what we called 'home' but left alone.

I fear she played the hard card well,

Divide and conquer, separate;

But I like to think we beat her hate,

At any rate, you're still the dearest brother

To me, both free and well, despite a young hell.

Roseanna Tyrell

OLD GHOSTS

Our old ghosts haunt the places we shared,

At shadows of the distant past,

I stared, in the home town where we walked hand in hand.

I look back with a life experience that has me

Sigh in resignation at my naivety and generosity

Of heart,

Remember how it smart, at that first betrayal;

Learning fast not to jump in with my heart;

A drawing of reigns on those emotions,

That tossed me in deep dark oceans,

In my youth.

I learned the many different shades of truth and lie

And I wonder why,

Life never makes things simpler, though you try.

I still seek that true love that will not die.

Roseanna Tyrell

FERNS ON THE HIGH BANK

Lush green fern fingers

Overhang a woody pathway

Their high stretch causing dappled light a way;

A graceful bouquet - a corsage for curly roots of trees;

Their 'fingers' catch the rays

And cause the cooling shade that weaves

A glory of delight,

Where lingers, beech nuts and last year's leaves

And eerie shadows.

All along the contrasts fight their way

Dark and light and into bright-

Where the trees end in the distance,

Their stance divine,

All along in line-

Fingery ferns seem to bob as if in adoration of the scene.

Summer 2015, in Cadamstown, behind Paddy Heaney's house.

Roseanna Tyrell

HONEYSUCKLE

Oh wild and wispy vine;

With a scent divine,

Delicate curling flutes,

With pinks both dark and pale

And creams to finish decoration of this lovely trail,

Of tiny, ox tongue textured licks

That entices the busy bee;

Fine threads of powdered stamen,

So miniscule and yet you see,

Damp and soft and perfumed

In the Sunday morning sun.

In and out the pretty vine twines

In a splendid run

Of carefree, windblown beauty

With no vanity to spoil,

Neither paint nor powder needed,

Just rain, and sun and soil.

A trail of subtle colour amid

The browns and greens,

Of a hedgerow in September this quiet beauty streams

2015

Roseanna Tyrell

PERICARPUS

With the shine and smoothness of a coffin, satin sash enclosed,

The chestnut case cracked in my hand;

The suck of the opening pod

Like the reverent muffledness of the tabernacle door

And the breeze sighs Nature's superiority of 'enclosure building';

Before man ever buried their dead in moneyed polished boxes, with sad white satin walls,

With carvings and a shiny dog-tag from the war of life - done and dusted.

The lock of the brown green prickly pod, without pin or screw to seal it fast

Leaves a question in the air about its design.

What cleverness is this that beats the brains of mankind, without mercy?

Its beginnings echoing the endings of man with superior ease and unfathomed wisdom?

Written after a chestnut fell in my path outside Ballinagar church, when I was working there at a funeral. 2014

Roseanna Tyrell

LIGHT FROM A BARGE

From the hump backed bridge, the yellow lit window of the barge

Shows a Spanish sunflower, warm, water world room of contentment and ease;

A man in bandana reads lost in yet another 'book' world.

I view this dimension in the dark, a window to past days.

To a book world, in this dizzy, busy rush haze,

Where time is slowed to the pace of the water clock, to heron stillness;

To the time of tea chests and the coal hump, billy cans and simplicity,

Or Sunday fishing, on a tree stump; but I'm dragged away by my world in a whirl of life.

(Inspired on seeing a barge as described above on my way home from Tullamore one night, late.)

Roseanna Tyrell

MY FATHER'S HANDS

Nearly always in movement,

Sure and strong,

Thick fingered, grasping lush green scallions

And flesh-tinted egg

In a rhythm of Sundays;

This ritual of movement,

Interspersed with the ceremony of sprinkling salt

From the blade of a too full knife tip,

Or else, it dipped deeply

Into the yellow of butter

Which began to dance

Along the hot knife

That had just divided the globe.

Sometimes pushing the curly handled plain,

Strong sure strokes,

His nicotine stained fingers

Sitting snugly in the grip;

Or moving swiftly through soft brown earth

Rescuing pale potatoes,

Throwing black dark sods,

Or swinging a sleán.

In rest, curling around a cigarette

Or as a prop for his jaw

In the round blue chair.

Often, I watched him in silence

Or bothered his ease

With a daring request for

A pound for school stuff;

A-feared to even touch that

Bump on the knuckle of his thumb,

This action showing too much love and care

In the cold eyes of my Mother.

(In memory of Da)

Roseanna Tyrell

PLOUGHING

A haven of delight, that view

from the hill field,

On a Spring morning dry and cold, the tradition old.

The tractor slow and steady

ploughs a furrow,

Straight as a die, with a fluttering audience on the fly;

In excitement, from the crow

down to the wren,

A vision of movement and life,

To stem hunger and strife;

The brown sod pungent, fresh and rich -

A seam of unearth meal -

Where seagulls squeal and twirl and twist -

Slow over places where the hard iron kissed;

In olden days quieter was that scene,

Just horse and man did toil below the bird flow;

As stones jarred and knocked against the plough toe.

The rattle of reins, Hey Up! and bird chatter

The only noises in the quiet morning field on a blue sky day.

Roseanna Tyrell

ROSES IN BALLINAGAR

A satin of rose leaves, under rose trees,

Yellows, pinks and reds,

The rose hips, fat and blushing, sunburnt,

In groups of bobbled 'pixie' heads;

'Hair' askew and full of dew, gems glitters here 'n there,

The impish crew, in fancy dress, cause one to stop and stare.

As if, an early morning party at young September's 'quest

The scene, in dew drop cobwebs decorated, sparkling, prettily dressed;

To honour fading beauties, with some satin gowns in tatters.

Some glory in last beauty,

Fresh with globes of past rain spatters;

A spindly spider hesitates, as if with fawning gentle touch.

To me this extant moment, shows Nature's elegance as such.

Roseanna Tyrell

Acknowledgements.

I wish to thank the members of Wordsmiths Tullamore for all their help, support and advice since the group was set up.

I would also like to thank all those who take the time to read my book. I hope you enjoy it.

SUSAN BOLAND

Biography

Susan Boland is a native of Co, Offaly; she was born and raised in Portarlington. (Offaly side of the bridge) She attended the local convent school where she gave the nuns a run for their money daily. Susan is the sixth child in a family of ten, she being the eldest girl. Susan has seven brothers and two sisters which led to a very wild, exciting and carefree childhood. Susan was a tomboy at heart and always got into the same mischief as the boys and loved it.

Susan grew up, got married and went on to have eight wonderful children. After successfully getting all her children to school one day and getting on with the household chores, words suddenly began to form in her head, swapping the sweeping brush for her computer, she put her words to text and from there her first poem was born, it was called The Housewife. After years of secretly writing and the children growing up she decided to see where her writing would take her and, on the advice of a friend, Susan joined a creative writing group and found a whole new writing family.

A collective decision was made to meet weekly to encourage and inspire each other and from there the Wordsmiths were born. A truly unique and talented bunch of people.

WALLOW DARK MEMORIES

Let me wallow in dark till I see the light.

Stand by my side through day and night.

Offer no words for they will not reach.

Just stand in silence in time I will seek.

Don't dry my tears, just let them flow.

Let the wetness seep into my soul.

Let me feel the pain that harbours the loss.

Of an innocent life, now an encumbering cross

An unwilling victim, yet I was saved.

I did withstand but I was never brave.

Let me feel the grief, let me wallow inside.

Envelope me with arms when I feel less alive.

Surround me with strength so I may feel renewed.

Embrace me with patience to help me navigate through.

Let my broken spirit sing to the sky above.

So, my heart can erase this loss with love.

Susan Boland

CHRONIC REPETITION

This chronic cocoon of repetition.

Visionally blinded, no admission.

Silently muted, no echo of sound.

Disfiguratively encased, tightly bound.

Cascading ripples loosely coiled.

Mutely flows, quietly wild.

Verbally auspicious, silently sound.

A raging fire meltingly drowns.

Subduction emotion, carelessly vile.

Unilaterally defended, emotionally soiled.

Perpetuating silence, stealthily fast.

The assistant anchor unsurpassed.

Unworthy the silence of repetition.

Uncase the grounding of definition.

Unwelcome the burden of muted silence.

Let the raging fire loose in this asylum.

Susan Boland

A LETTER FROM ANGEL

Hi Mommy,

Please don't be sad,

I'm safe here in heaven with great-granddad.

God said, "Angel you must come with me".

I was not meant for this world Mommy.

I was not meant to be.

God said you needed an angel to watch over you,

He put me on his lap and said this is what you must do.

Go visit your Mommy when she is asleep

Tell her you love her as you place a kiss on her cheek.

God told me to tell you it was not your fault

He said do not feel guilty there was no cause.

I feel your sadness as you cry and weep.

I'm here in your heart Mommy, just feel my beat.

Please dry your eyes and do not cry,

I may not have lived, yet I did not die.

God gave me wings so I could fly,

To help me always be by your side.

Please, be happy Mommy and Daddy too.

For I will always be watching over you.

Susan Boland

MY TINY DANCER

My tiny dancer with big shoes to fill

Transport me back to a time that will.

Help me remember the chastity of youth

When I could breach, unveil and execute.

Help me tap out the memories of days

When a consummate mission could perpetrate

The energy as we glissade across the floor

The tune as it is tapped out upon the board.

My memory has long ago forgotten the words

But my soul still remembers the tunes it heard

My feet on their own have found free will

You gave me that moment to feel the thrill.

My tiny dancer, my beautiful child

Dance me some happiness for a little while

Transcend me tapping to the beat that thrilled

My tiny dancer, what big shoes you have filled

Susan Boland

A SHADOWED ABYSS

I'm in a void with darkness or light

There is no day, there is no night

I don't feel happy, I don't feel sad

I don't do chatty, I don't feel mad

I tell no truths, I tell no lie.

I say no hellos or no goodbyes

My eyes are dry, I do not cr.

I don't feel alive, yet I did not die

My eyes are open, yet I cannot see

I don't move my hands to try to fee.

I don't want to breathe to fill my lung.

Or sing a song that's already been sung

I don't walk a mile in any one's shoes

I don't really care if that's an excuse

I don't have a business that's my own

I don't want company, leave me alone

I do not care if you want to try

I've lost it all, now let me die.

Susan Boland

A CONSCIOUS THOUGHT

Never the twain shall we discover

The catacomb of insanity the lies unrecovered

Never a thought shall we reign as rationality

For the conscious thought has no nationality.

A thought diluted by memory interrupted

As sanity frees itself from the corrupted

A momentary thought, a judgement lapsed

The insanity of a conscious mind now collapsed.

No dormant mind can infringe on insanity

No conversation can claim it's just anxiety

No rendering truths of madness uncovered

Yet sanity can be masked or silently smothered.

A uniform silence for the trial of insanity

Masters the conscious thought of inhumanity

For insanity rules what can never be bought

After all, sanity is just a conscious thought.

Susan Boland

THE GOLDEN THREAD OF DECEPTION

The thread that holds is starting to fray.

It falls piece by piece as it begins to sway.

No glue can bound the thread like tares.

For the thread that holds, weaves no cares.

A delicate tension, neither loose or tight.

Like an endless day without a night.

The urge to pull the tension fraught

The thread that holds could not be caught.

To weave a thread for one that strong.

To hold and bind the forever wrongs.

Like a spider who spins a web of gold.

Like a fly who enters, it entraps its soul.

The golden thread runs steel underneath.

It will not be bent to meet the needs.

It runs a course of singular intention.

An ominous golden thread of deception.

Susan Boland

A CHILD OF SYRIA

I was a child of Syria, innocent of my birth

I was an outcast to the world; I'm now entombed in dirt

You stole from me my future, no choices were my own

You dropped a bomb and killed me, it's evil you have sown

The poison gas fell on my skin, at first I thought it rained

My eyes they closed all by themselves,

My life force slowly drained

I was a child of Syria, a simple child of eight

Who never understood what it was to hate

My life on earth it ended, but I did not go alone

My Mother lay beside me, lifeless in a hole

I was a child of Syria who wanted to live a life

Who wanted to be happy, free from terror and from strife?

Will the world ever remember that I was just a child?

I was just a child of Syria, exiled and defiled

So, to the powers that hold our lives in their hands

Remember, it was by your command I was killed on my land.

Susan Boland

A SILENT SIGH

A tearful cry, yet no path claimed.

A silent sigh, no breath taken.

A silent word, yet it screamed.

One holy person here but unseen.

A silent prayer but for who's ear.

A distance so great, no one can hear.

A falling sensation, there is no ground.

It falls like a rock, but makes no sound.

A speech is given, no one hears the words.

They are deaf and dumb in their own world.

That tearful cry has claimed its wrath.

As that silent sigh just follows its path.

The sound of silence, no one breaks.

That passage in time, no one takes.

A perfect world looks good from inside.

They did not realise they had died.

Susan Boland

A SILENT WAR

A Silent soldier behind the scene.

A silent war unheard and unseen.

A silent scream no ear can hear.

And upon its face, one single tear.

The silent soldier stands his ground

As war, it rages all around.

The silent casualties no one can place.

A silent culture, no creed, no race.

The silent words that will never convey

To the silent soldier that stands in their way.

Of the invisible footprints of a bloody war.

Steeped in ashes death and gore.

So silently do they close their eyes.

No vision of death or where they lie.

The silence of death will it ever cease?

Will the silent soldier ever find peace?

Susan Boland

A POMPOUS ASS

Gesticulating in one's own greatness.
Commanding the presence of acquaintance.
The bombastic assumption is ostentatious.
The embodiment of one's influential greatness.

A paramount of considerable pomposity.
With reference to one's educational odyssey.
Relaying the absence of unapologetic modesty.
Exalting in advance of one's own priority.

Victoriously accomplished, a conquest conquered.
Unlimited access, a proclamation offered.
No apprehension of intermediary class.
No resolution, the proclamation crass.

Richly affluent, flamboyantly flash.
A very presumptuous pompous ass.
Egotism in honour of self-admiration.
Assured in self-confidence and gratification.

Susan Boland

THE RHYTHM OF LIFE

If we were perfect, we would never strive.

We could never discern if we were wrong or right.

To always succeed and never endeavour,

To aspire and battle to always be greater.

The exasperation of failure is a rung of success.

A learned capability to acquire nothing less.

The survival in life is fraught with failure.

Yet failure is the teacher that becomes our saviour.

The journey of failing is the measure of growing.

We fail, we rise, and we keep on going.

Each time we fail is a lesson learned.

And a lesson learned in one we have earned.

Don't fear the future we cannot foresee.

Take it one step at a time, slowly breathe.

Failure is not failure when you have given your all.

It's the rhythm of life, we rise, and we fall.

This next poem is in remembrance of our fellow wordsmith and friend, whom we miss more than we ever thought possible.

Susan Boland

CAMILLUS BOLAND

Your strength shone through till the bitter end.

Our lives were richer we got to call you friend.

You always inspired with words and rhymes.

Knowing life could take you at any time.

Ah Camillus you loved to laugh and sing.

Compose your words about different things.

You always left us with a tear or a smile.

With words that were always caring and kind.

You always accepted what was to be your fate.

And with strength and courage you bore that weight.

But God saw you struggle and said it was time.

Time to go home Camillus where you will forever shine.

Susan Boland

THE SILENCE

Listen with ears that hear no sound,

See with eyes, that's hidden and bound.

Touch with fingers tips, yet do not feel.

Speak with silence that can never heal.

Embrace the love one cannot reveal.

Conform to change to help repeal.

Observe covertly and welcome reprieve.

And with open arms continuously receive.

Harmonize the stillness to stay in tune.

Rectify the chaos to discontinue the ruin.

Never surrender the legitimacy of truth.

Never conform let silence be the root.

Unite and conquer the silent crusades.

To combat the horror of sharpened blades.

Seek revelation and cause for procurement.

To heal the silence to counter the movement.

Susan Boland

THE DIRTY SMUTS

Don't touch those chimneys, the dirty smuts.

They need the sweeps to clean their soot's.

Up they climb, brush on their back.

And upon the roof they lay their sacks.

Brush in hand as they make the stand.

Ready to poke at the chimney band.

Scrape it good and scrape it well.

And leave no soot for her to tell.

Who heats her fire, I will not say?

For it is steam she pumps out every day.

She gets so hot she starts to boil.

It doesn't last long its only oil.

The chimney is cleaned, the sweeps did poke.

They are all now ready for a good puff of smoke.

So, stack her well and stack her high.

As she expels her smoke into the sky.

Susan Boland

A SWAGGERING REFLECTION

Drink ye the memories of thy youth

When ye boys were boisterous and ye men uncouth.

A kingdom to reign, be it only in name

Thy memories of youth, now old and inflamed.

Oh, sorrowful woes of a timely time.

Death's a knocking and the grim reaper shines.

Come forth ye and listen of my tale to tell

Afore the grim reaper takes me straight to hell.

Upon a time when youth was kind

And my bounty of riches, richly mined.

But age is the curse as the bones grow weak

And my faith is meeting me as I speak.

My bottles of whiskey, sugar and rum.

Are hiding in a cave dry, in a drum.

I'll give ye the map of where it is stashed.

Cross my hand with silver and let us not hash.

I'll buy me some rum and drink me to hell.

While I fall into the fiery pits of my cell.

I smuggled and sold my cargo and wares.

When I was young and bold, and devil may care.

Susan Boland

CONSEQUENSES OF LIFE

A river flows

Sand blows

Water is the balm to earth's dry throat

The sun scorches

The rays burn

Our seasons have begun to turn

The soil it dries and falls like dust

Our trees they wither away in disgust

Our mountains fall from their proudest peaks

Our lands disappearing beneath our feet.

The wind it howls in angry gales

Lets loose what's tied like ocean sails

It cannot count what walks the earth

It savagely unveils what's left in dearth

The pits of fire rise slowly to the fore

They thunderously explode with a mighty roar

The rains that follow will enormously swallow

Till all we can do is stand and wallow.

We kill what we need in this life to survive

Our consequences of life will then be denied

We need to awaken and repeal the lies.

OUR EARTH IS IN TROUBLE WE EITHER SAVE IT OR IT DIES.

Susan Boland

THE OPIATE OF SOCIETY.

Verbiciously sweetened with the nectar of honey

With a protruding lie, spiking it with money.

Richly affluent who charismatically blends

An opiate of society, a fashionable friend.

Characteristically obese with the propensity to sway.

To romanticize and magnify ,to overestimate.

A declaration of truth, they will never deny

The disproportionate opiate shrouded in lies.

A contaminate in society, sequestered in wealth.

A masked occult, esoterically stealth.

A mass induction, a secreted installation.

The commencement and birth, of a new creation.

Audaciously aggressive with influential compatriots.

A supposition to demand, the craving to insatiate.

In anticipation of a reasonable persuasion.

A conviction to give credence to the expectation.

Susan Boland

THE COBBLED ROAD

Strength is born when endurance is tested.

The cobbled road has beaten and infected.

Weariness shatters the fortitude gathered.

An expulsion of feeling that no longer matters.

The voice of heart battles with the soul.

The journey fraught upon the cobbled road.

The senses awaken to what lies ahead.

Endurance is found when strength is dead.

The heart still beats its pounding fierce.

The soul it screams so loud it can pierce.

The cobbled road endeavours to defy.

The life that beats so wildly inside.

The cracks of endurance the scars of conflict.

The adversity constant and eager to inflict.

The cobbled road unrelenting and cruel.

The strength of endurance endured and grew.

Susan Boland

WISTFUL WHISPERS

In the night time shadows I hear their thoughts

Like whimsical dreams that can never be caught

Like feathers that float on the gentle breeze

Flitting and floating down with ease

Wistful whispers, sighing gently upon my ears

A verbal chorus of unwritten tears.

Their lives expired their memories lapsed

Their stories unwritten their time now passed.

On a sigh of words their stories lament

With staggered breaths their lives they rent.

A listening conduit, their words unfold

As graceful hands their stories compose

The blemished whispers of tarnished lives

Their anguished cries of lives destroyed

Their whispered words, a message from above

Treat all human-kind with respect and love.

Susan Boland

Acknowledgements

To the listening ears of my family I love you all beyond words. I need to mention my crazy grandchildren who constantly make me laugh and always brighten my days. I am truly blessed.

To the library staff in Tullamore thank you, there is always a smile and a helping hand when one is needed. And thank you for your constant support I really appreciate it.

To my Wordsmiths family who are a truly unique and talented bunch who inspire, encourage and give me the confidence to continue with my writing journey. Thank you peeps I would be lost without you. I so love my writing family.

Now Vincent don't grumble this is well deserved because you always seem to know the right words to say when we need them. You are a true gentleman and thank you for always having a kind word.

LORRAINE; there is so much goodness in you it should be packaged and sent all around the world, what a cheerful place it would be then, you have committed an enormous amount of your time and work to help us all out. SERIOUSLY I don't think thank you is a big enough word for what you do. I love the bones of you. Thank you xx

To Pauline Mc Namee who facilitated my very first creative writing course where you proceeded to give me permission to write badly thereby releasing me of any pressure, many, many thanks.

To G my friend, whose advice pointed me in the right direction thank you.